Short Story International

SHORT STORY INTERNATIONAL

Tales by the World's
Great Contemporary Writers
Presented Unabridged

All selections in
Short Story International
are reprinted full and
unabridged in the author's
own words. Nothing is
added, subtracted,
condensed or rewritten.

Editor
Sylvia Tankel

Associate Editor
Erik Sandberg-Diment

Contributing Editor
John Harr

Assistant Editors
Mildred Butterworth
Arlene Loveless
Kirsten Hammerle

Art Director
Mort Rubenstein

Circulation Director
Nat Raboy

Production Director
Ludwig K. Marz

Business Manager
John O'Connor

Publisher
Sam Tankel

Volume 7, Number 37, April 1983
Short Story International (USPS 375-970)
Copyright © by International Cultural
Exchange 1983. Printed in the U.S.A. All
rights reserved. Reproduction in whole or in
part prohibited. Second-class postage paid
at Great Neck, N.Y. 11022 and at additional
mailing offices. **Editorial offices: P.O. Box
405, Great Neck, N.Y. 11022.** Enclose
stamped, self-addressed envelope with
previously published stories submitted for
possible reprinting in *Short Story
International*. Please note *SSI* does not
accept unpublished original manuscripts.
One year (six issues) subscription for U.S.,
U.S. possessions $16, Canada $18 (US),
other countries $21 (US). All institutions add
$2 per annual subscription. Single copy
price $3.45. **For subscriptions and
address changes write to Short Story
International. P.O. Box 405, Great Neck,
N.Y. 11022.** *Short Story International* is
published bimonthly by International
Cultural Exchange, 6 Sheffield Road, Great
Neck, N.Y. 11021. Postmaster please send
Form 3579 to P.O. Box 405, Great Neck,
N.Y. 11022.

Note from the Editor

Our incoming mail, responding to the change in our cover design introduced with *Short Story International* No. 35, was not unanimous. Four subscribers took exception.

In the heavy flow of laudatory mail, two positive suggestions repeatedly surfaced: that *SSI* be published more frequently, and that we increase the number of stories in our issues.

This issue reflects our endorsement for additional stories. We have positioned the stories so that one directly follows another, eliminating illustrations which had taken space we now allot for more stories.

It is an old story that change is a constant. At *SSI* change augments our affection for the short story and increases our pleasure in the growing recognition of the short story as the mainstay of literature.

Copyrights and acknowledgments

We wish to express deep thanks to the authors, publishers, translators and literary agents for their permission to publish the stories in this issue.

"A Promise to Settle" by Ian Nash first appeared in *The Australian*. Copyright Ian Nash. "A Shot of Damascus" from *Valid For All Countries* by Desmond O'Grady. Copyright © 1979 Desmond O'Grady. "Mrs. CMS" from *Daughters of an Ancient Race* by Jack Reynolds. Copyright © 1974 Jack Reynolds. By permission of Heinemann Educational Books (Asia) Ltd. "An Empty Bed" by Yehia Hakki, from a collection edited by the American University, translated by Mahmoud Manzalaoui, revised by Leonard Knight and Lewis Hall. Copyright Yehia Hakki. By permission of the author. "Summer and Miss Swanson" from *The Darling Fishes & Other Tales of Fantasy, Horror and the Supernatural* by Rick Ferreira. Copyright © 1979 Rick Ferreira. Published by William Kimber. "A Kind of Madness" by E.G. Chipulina, 1983. "The Name" by Aharon Megged from *Israeli Stories*, ed. Joel Blocker. Translation by Minna Givton. Copyright © 1962 Schocken Books, Inc. "A Short Visit" by Yukiko Hirota, 1983. "By Acclamation" by Francis Ebejer, 1983. "Just a Mild-Mannered Man" by Olive Winchester, 1983. "A Doll" by Martijne van Laar. Copyright © 1981. M.G. van Laar. "The Frog Lady" from *The Itinerary of Beggars* by H.E. Francis originally appeared in *Prairie Schooner*. Copyright © 1956 the University of Nebraska Press. By permission of the author and *Prairie Schooner*. "Uncle's Bargain" by Yale Sussman first appeared in *Find*. Copyright 1981 Yale Sussman. "The Lie" by Anatoly Alexin, translation by L. Flaxman. By permission of VAAP.

Photo credits: Yale Sussman by Charles Elioseff. Anatoly Alexin by Vladimir Savostyanov. © Sovfoto.

Table of Contents

"She'd reached the stage where she was lost without him, now it seemed she was beginning to be lost with him."

A Promise to Settle

BY IAN NASH

RETURNING to their trailer, John was surprised to find that Marianne wasn't there.

Certainly he was back later than usual. The wind, which usually rose in the heat of late afternoon to fill the stifling vacuum, had blown more strongly this afternoon, and after work he'd made his way through familiar rows of apricots, oranges and vines towards the river.

He'd watched the Murray ripple and flurry darkly, pricked at points by a few heavy raindrops. But there had been no storm. The wind seemed to have forgotten what it had started and, vaguely disappointed, John turned back.

The vines that had been yesterday's work and laughter and talk and sweat were now torn and stripped of their plumpness, the faint gold of the leaves becoming old yellow. So he'd taken the long way around in order to pass through those rows of vines that bulged still with promise.

But Marianne ought to be here.

"Marianne!" he called.

She hadn't even started to prepare their evening meal. He couldn't understand it. It was most unlike her to go to see anyone at this time. And she was afraid of the orchards at night.

He called again, fairly bellowing this time.

A stone's throw away, propped against the scaly trunk of one of the old apricot trees, Marianne sat ripping leaves to dwindling shapes and burying her feet in the cooling sand. She knew he was back, had heard him call for her.

But she'd been waiting for him for hours and she was tired of being there every time he wanted her, existing only when he wanted or remembered her. He'd laugh, she knew, if she told him she didn't feel needed any more; he'd treat it as the old-age woman fancy and laugh till she was convinced she was silly.

She'd reached the stage where she was lost without him, now it seemed she was beginning to be lost with him.

"Marianne!"

She'd waited for hours for him and now he expected her to come running. Her back pained as she drew herself up. Four years in fact she'd been waiting—waiting for him to call an end to the whole futile business. She was drying up in this sun that had become too much of a good thing, aching for no good reason. John couldn't see that, he couldn't see that the picking and the heat really took it out of her body. He couldn't see that she'd had enough of pretending they'd escaped the rat race.

He was searching the cupboards for something to eat as she stepped into the van.

"Where have you been?"

It was a demand more than concern and she resented the air of proprietorship.

"Walking."

He bent to kiss her, to heal all with the magic touch. His mouth was almost on her when she jerked her head sharply to one side so that he kissed the air.

"What's the matter?"

"I've got to get dinner.

He stepped back to let her move, but continued to watch her, hovering above and behind her.

"Tired?"

She shot him a look that banked a flood of words. He was determined to be wronged and words would only complicate things.

"A bit," she replied.

He continued to hover, watching her.

"Why don't you sit down?"

But he wouldn't leave her side, had to watch for some chink in the face that refused to admit him by storm.

"But I've told you before," he began in the most reasonable of tones, "you don't have to pick every day. Take a day off now and then if you get so tired." He paused. "You don't have to pick at all if it comes to that."

She'd have to say more now, before he talked her into being the whole trouble with herself and enough to cause him misery too. "It's not that." She turned away from him, struggling to retain her distance and the sound of reason. "Not just that, anyway."

"What then?"

She flung up her arms. "I can't move in here!"

The touch of hysteria was a mistake. He moved in with suffocating sympathy.

"Tell me now. What's really the matter?"

She looked at him resentfully, and in the same instant despairing—looking past him.

"What's the use?"

It was his turn to throw up his hands. "God!" So much for the patient, concerned husband. His voice dropped, retreating from the snarl into a familiar sort of choking.

"You want a house, rose bushes and babies. Right?"

She ignored the scorn. "There's such a thing as waiting too long for something. By the time you get it, it doesn't mean anything."

"You want me in collar and tie, carrying my empty briefcase and riding some stinking suburban train morning and night."

"It doesn't have to be..."

"Buy you a house and sell myself as part of the bargain."

11

"Sell yourself! What's to sell? Just take a look at some of your fruit picking buddies out there. Take a good long look and see yourself— a real bum! Another gutless wonder!"

Her head reeled to the sudden thud of his hand on her jaw. She dropped the plates she was holding and, wheeling blindly, pushed past him and out of the van, the screen door banging and flailing behind her.

She'd barely reached the shadow of the nearest trees when she heard the door bang again. He was coming after her. But she made no effort to run faster; already she was pushing herself against a host of frightening shapes that loomed and moved all about her. She hadn't realized it was so late. Orange trees she thought she knew, cool and friendly in the heat of day, were massive, threatening strangers; the old apricots that arched like a chapel had become a tunnel of quivering shadows.

She was almost glad to reach the dark waves of vines that were her torment by day; here she could at least feel her head and shoulders free of the shapes and darkness that threatened to drown her.

But she was tired of running. The sand felt like gum under her shoes and she shivered as though the freshness of the night were already the chill of morning. If he caught her she would have to stop, she hadn't the strength to go on. She could hear his breath, his feet in the sand. Yet it seemed he'd never reach her, so that her knees felt weak with running and waiting.

She stumbled, and pitched forward with a sudden weight behind her—his weight pressing her into the sand. And then he was touching, lifting, turning her head.

"Come on now. I'm sorry."

Breathless and sobbing she allowed her chin to sink into the firmness of his hand.

"It's all right." He caressed her face with his. "It's all right now."

But she'd sob no matter what he said or did. He could stop her talking, stop her running, but he had to let her sob.

"I didn't mean it. I know what you meant. Honest I do. And I'm sorry."

She averted her head, not fighting him, but determined not to be easy.

"Sorry? For what?"

"For everything."

She'd have asked for more, to hear him say exactly what he repented and be that much surer of him; but his mouth had begun to play over her face, warm and gently furrowing—pushing up over her cheeks and into her eyelids until she was forgetful and falling. Falling back from the weight that had come to the front of her, ever so gently, then persistently easing her back into the sand.

"No! No don't! Not here."

"Why not?"

"It's...it's too light. The moon..."

"You want children, don't you?"

His words were soft, the idea brutal, coldly closing over her little protest as though it had never existed. Her body stiffened as she found herself confronted at once by that which she wanted most and—things being as they were and as she'd seen them over the last four years—the very thing she might live to regret. She held him away, her fist tight in his chest.

"No! No, not if they're going to be pickers' kids."

For an instant she was afraid he might laugh. But he knew the kids she meant, had watched and pitied them himself. The sort who missed too much school, played aimlessly in the sand around the vines, clinging to parents who seemed always too tired and too insubstantial to have them cling.

"No, of course not. Don't be silly."

"Promise. Promise me," her knuckles hard in his chest.

"I promise," he breathed, and felt her fist relax and collapse beneath him.

Which left only a specter between them.

"I promise, I promise, I promise," he murmured, to push it further and further away until, in time with their beautiful motion, he'd willed all "pickers' kids" forever out of existence.

 *Ian Nash was born in Yea, Victoria, in 1942. After completing an Art degree at Melbourne University, he taught for several years. He has published numerous short stories, many of which have been anthologized. His play* Blood Brothers *was produced in Melbourne.*

"...Damascus had made an overwhelming
impression on Phelan: he felt he had been hit
by a blast from the furnace of revolution."

A Shot of Damascus

BY DESMOND O'GRADY

AS the shout had made Phelan's finger jump on the shutter, the
resulting photograph would be askew. He swore at the busybody
across the bridge and wound the key of his old camera as a
preliminary to another shot of the minaret with its witch's hat spires.

The fellow who had shouted was still staring hostilely at him, but
Phelan counted on the tacit protection of the occasional passers-by
and the soldier on duty at the other end of the bridge. However, as
he focused again, the squat fellow crossed toward him barking
reproof. His bullish head was not quite level with Phelan's shoulder.
His thinning hair reminded Phelan of a laurel wreath as its tufts
pointed in all directions along the rim of a forehead which was
sweaty, even though it was a mild, spring afternoon. Phelan
wondered whether he could handle the fellow if it came to a fight: he
feared the busybody might butt.

Phelan spoke English, French and Italian without getting through to his censor, who kept up his quickfire Arabic as if the force of it, together with his outsize expressions and gestures, would penetrate the foreigner's dull brain. The soldier and the passers-by were indifferent to the confrontation.

Phelan leaned the small of his back against the bridge's parapet, tucked his camera protectively under one arm, and waited for the excited citizen to simmer down. He was gesturing toward the minaret, and as Phelan followed the gesture he saw that military trucks were parked in the courtyard alongside it. Did the busybody, who was now inviting him to walk off the bridge, imagine that he was photographing a military installation? But, if this was the case, why should he be upset rather than the soldier at the far end of the bridge?

Abruptly the vigilante pulled a pistol from the pocket of his leather jacket and Phelan's air of patient superiority vanished. For all the interest the soldier and the passers-by showed, as Phelan quickly noted, the pistol might have been a cigarette, and he suspected that it was empty. But he feared, nevertheless, that a bullet might rend the scene's unreality and his tender flesh. His lower back was suddenly cold, his nonchalance dissolved and he obediently accompanied the gunman off the bridge.

Phelan did not want to die in Damascus. He was not even on duty: he had journalistic assignments in several Middle East countries but Syria was not one of them. He had merely taken the opportunity to stop over in Damascus as a tourist, which was why he had been photographing the witch's hat minarets.

As a journalist he rarely took photographs. He was scornful of people who spent their travels slicing the world into a little box. His camera reflected this attitude and an assumption that a humanist must be incompetent with the latest mechanical gadgets. It was a vintage Kodak Brownie with an expandable image box.

Phelan had no need of a camera except to take photographs of, and for, his two children, for he himself was a camera. It was not merely that he had an exact visual memory; journalism had aggravated his natural tendency to record everything as a detached observer.

Coming off the bridge, he folded the bellows back and snapped the camera shut, reassuring his suspicious guard at the same time with sign language. The Syrian had slipped the gun back in his pocket and, satisfied that the foreigner was cowed, walked alongside him exuding an irksome self-righteousness and an odor which was part heavy perfume, part sour sweat. Instead of entering the courtyard where the military trucks were parked, the pair took the tree-lined street which was a continuation of the bridge, with Phelan reflecting that, in other circumstances, he would have enjoyed the walk.

Since his arrival the previous day, Damascus had made an overwhelming impression on Phelan: he felt he had been hit by a blast from the furnace of revolution. The dynamism of the city was bracing. All the buses, driven with an abandon which was proof of faith in Allah, had radios blaring at a deafening pitch. Martial music and impassioned speeches, which were the radio's sole fare, swept though the city with the buses. At street corners, television sets on high stands showed military men, chests laden with decorations, delivering emphatic speeches. Bookstands overflowed with publications such as *Peking News*. A stiff wind scoured the sky of clouds and held the hosts of green-starred red, white and black flags taut.

At night, on the hills overlooking the city, a huge neon sign lit up whose Arabic was translated for Phelan as "Long Live the Socialist Revolution."

In the afternoon he had watched a procession celebrating the achievements of Socialism: sputniks and other spacecraft occupied the major floats. Background to the jammering propaganda was the intact ancient city, with crowded market and empty mosque, to which had been added what would pass as an attractive French provincial town.

Phelan had observed pairs of soldiers walking hand in hand; he had lingered in the mosque where one of John the Baptist's heads was kept; he had eaten unidentifiable but delicious food in a small restaurant; he had walked by the swift-flowing river lined with neat French-style, glass-fronted restaurants; he had come to the bridge, noted with delight the witch's hat spires and had decided he would return to photograph them for his children.

I could have drawn the minarets for them, he told himself, as he strode beside his captor. Phelan tried once more to establish communication in scraps of several languages, then, finding that the Syrian was deaf to them all, he told him, in the most conciliatory tone possible, that he was an interfering, officious prig, that he should stop trying to live up to Syrian stereotypes or be booked for overacting.

They had reached the outskirts of the city and the Syrian was explaining something in his staccato manner. Evidently he was telling the tall, sandy-haired foreigner that they had reached their destination, for they turned into an asphalted courtyard where groups of men stood chatting. Some of them greeted the captor as if he were a hunter returned with a good bag. Taking Phelan by the arm, he half-helped, half-pushed him through a doorway. Here, a phlegmatic official, who ignored all Phelan's attempts to talk to him, took down the captor's account of events, then dismissed him.

Phelan felt the better for that. Now all he wanted was someone to whom he could explain the whole ridiculous episode. He was passed to a surly, slow-moving official who understood Phelan's faltering French but was skeptical of his explanation that, even though his passport showed he was a journalist, he was in Damascus as a mere tourist.

When the official told Phelan that he would have to refer the case to his superior, it increased the journalist's annoyance and aroused his anxiety. He realized that it may have sounded a little odd that he should be merely sightseeing in Syria, but decided to stick to the truth as he lazily thought himself beyond suspicion. He was reminding himself that he was the one who should be demanding an explanation from the authorities when he was summoned upstairs to Captain Khahil's bare office. As soon as Khahil introduced himself Phelan forgot about being a ruffled tourist and summoned his journalistic awareness: the interview would be a tough one. Khahil's ramrod back held him only at a medium height but he had cool authority and spoke an exquisite French which put Phelan at a disadvantage. He had an aura of calm as if he moved and had his being on an isolated pinnacle. His spotless uniform must have been tailored for his slim figure: it was a sheer blue linen and as elegant as his movements which seemed rehearsed to perfection.

His eyes, too, were blue and quizzical, and dominated an acute, ascetic face. He read through the report of the incident, sitting rigidly at his tidy desk with lips pursed, like a headmaster. He asked Phelan for the camera and, when he did not succeed in opening the ancient contraption, handed it back, inviting Phelan to give him the film. "I hope they are not of high artistic quality," Khahil said facetiously.

Phelan told himself that it was probably a security officer's idea of a pleasantry and decided to play it very cool. He wanted to avoid handing over the film for the good reason that it had some identifiably Israeli shots on it, of the Sea of Galilee and Nazareth, taken solely for the children, of course. He was thoroughly alive, at last, to the implausibility of his story from the Syrian official's viewpoint. Phelan had traveled with double passports, one for Israel and one for the Arab countries, but he did not fancy explaining to the suspicious Khahil how he had shots of Israel when the passport shown on entry to Syria indicated only that he had visited Arab countries.

Stalling for time, he asked whether it was forbidden to take photographs of mosques or of military establishments and was told it was forbidden to take photographs "of the city." He thought of touching a pathetic note by saying the photographs were for his children but Captain Khahil hardly seemed open to sentimental appeals. Phelan feared that any further delay in handing over the film would count against him when, once it was developed, he was called to explain the Israeli shots.

Khahil wound an elastic band around the film and placed it in the tray beside him with the precision of a surgeon. Phelan's mind was racing now, but on closed circuit; he was circumcised but, if it was discovered, how could he explain it was a common practice in Australia, that he was a Catholic of dependable Irish extraction and not a filthy Israeli spy who had entered Syria under false pretenses? If only there were an Irish pastor in Damascus to put him through the hoops so that he could prove his orthodoxy. He still had the penny catechism off by heart. Who is God? Allah. He saw himself stripped before Syrian judges, condemned for his telltale sexual organ, crucified for a faith he did not even share.

Phelan knew he had to hide the collapse of his confidence by making a show of offended innocence. He protested about the overbearing fellow who had arrested him, asking what was his authority.

Steepling his small hands, Khahil explained that the fellow was only a private citizen who may have been carried away by his zeal, but added that he was a patriot. "In these days," he said, as if challenging Phelan to contradict him, "we are all patriots to guarantee the security of the nation; soon all the enemies of Syria will be hanged."

Captain Khahil was explaining that he looked forward to that day, for it would allow him to return to Aleppo, but Phelan was only half-listening, worried lest his face reflect his inner turmoil. He was thinking of the decorated tile from the Jerusalem Mosque of Omar which lay at the bottom of his traveling bag. He cursed his irresponsibility; if discovered, he would look foolish as well as reckless.

He had slipped the blue-patterned tile under his coat as soon as he arrived at the Mosque of Omar, picking it from the fragments scattered during repairs to the building's ceramic frieze. It was not for the children: he intended to add it to the other curious fragments, acquired in similar ways, which decorated the terrace of his Roman apartment. But more than his magpie instincts were involved: it had also been a silly sort of adventure, a muffled echo of Christians going in disguise on pilgrimage to Mecca. An Arab urchin who had seen him was a potential threat, but Phelan had slipped him some baksheesh, visited the mosque, whose interior did not match its superb exterior, and succeeded in carrying the tile past the guards at the compound entrance.

Phelan had had a moment's fear when a brusque customs official at Damascus airport had gone through his traveling bag, but the tile was not found, buried as it was in Phelan's soiled clothing. Phelan had his response ready if he were challenged about it: it was merely a stray tile which had taken his fancy.

He was less comfortable about it now, however: could he stick to that bland answer if they were shouting at him that it was a sacrilegious theft from one of Islam's holiest shrines where Mohammed had taken flight for heaven?

This very minute, Phelan told himself in silent panic, all the greater for his earlier excessive nonchalance, Captain Khahil's men could well be routing through his things at the Letakia Hotel, digging out the tile, his second airline ticket, which was further proof that he had been to Israel, and even his copy of Muriel Spark's novel *The Mandelbaum Gate* which they might regard as a manual for spies. Phelan warned himself that Captain Khahil probably considered him as a threat to the nation: in a madhouse, he reflected, the sane are counted crazy.

Khahil was giving a reasonable explanation of the reigning unreason: that extraordinatry measures were necessary in an emergency.

"It would be unfortunate if you got the wrong impression, Monsieur Phelan," he said gravely, implying that it would be only M. Phelan's fault if he did, "for even though you say you are here as a tourist you are, of course, a journalist."

And a circumcised one at that, Phelan added under his breath.

"You say you live in Rome," the captain continued in a way which may have been merely conversational but could also express doubts about all Phelan's affirmations.

Phelan said that he had a Roman wife.

The impeccable captain thawed. "Mediterranean people are the best," he said, throwing his arms wide. "Hitler was wrong in that. I don't think he was an historian of good academic standing." He wrinkled his nose.

Phelan had no difficulty in agreeing. Khahil, pointing out in his chiseled French that Mussolini had done more than Hitler to liberate the Middle East from the French and English yoke, said he admired the Italians but for the fact that they had hanged Mussolini. He hurried on to say that Hitler, whom he had seen delivering speeches when, as a student, he had visited Germany from Paris, also had great merits.

Phelan guessed correctly that the first one was his Jewish policy. He objected mildly that this had not endeared Hitler to the Western world, but Khahil, in the tone of a man stating a truism, answered that the West was hypocritical.

Hitler's other great merit, according to Khahil, was to ensure order and discipline. "Only when the Arabs regain order and discipline will they once again be a great people," he concluded, as if he were the first to make such a comment.

Phelan felt he must advance a reserve to hide his unease. He asked whether discipline could be attained if, as he had found, citizens were allowed to threaten innocent people.

Khahil enjoyed the objection. He smiled remotely at the benighted liberal in his power, went to a cabinet under the window and extracted a bottle of Pernod.

"You're right to worry about uncontrolled violence, Monsieur Phelan," he said, pouring out two measures of the pineapple yellow liquid, "but here it is a question of controlled violence. I appreciate your feelings toward that fellow. But he is made to feel that he is participating in the revolution. Don't worry: he is under control. Those who go beyond a certain limit are hanged—and everybody knows it."

Phelan wanted to know how many were hanged each month.

Captain Khahil was very much at his ease. He drew a pale blue handkerchief from his jacket sleeve and dabbed slowly at his temples and upper lip. There was a whiff of scent, but it was far more discreet than that worn by Phelan's captor.

"What sense would figures have?" he asked, and lingered over his Pernod as if waiting for Phelan's answer before continuing. "People here have always been hanged. The novelty is that now they're hanged only for clear reasons and only to form a disciplined people."

Phelan sat unconvinced, thinking of his circumcision, his fragment of the Mosque of Omar, and whether he would meet the fate of those who overstepped their limits, Khahil's penchant for talking about hanging seemed unhealthy. Phelan regarded his Pernod as the suave offering made by police chiefs in second-rate adventure fiction before throwing their victims into solitary cells.

"You're familiar with Sorel, no doubt, Monsieur Phelan," said Khahil. Phelan came to with a start and his mind flicked to the French film star Jean Sorel, but then, in a misty recess of memory, he identified the reference to the philosopher of violence. Phelan's

French conversation was highly stylized, limited to a small vocabulary and fixed forms. He had been pleasantly surprised to find that Khahil, unlike many Frenchmen, did not make him conscious of its shortcomings. His cramped style was now a help in hiding his ignorance. He ventured the safe opinion that no one had really put Sorel's ideas into action, then led on to Mussolini and Malaparte's works. He was, he told himself, home and hosed. Khahil was still riding his hobbyhorse and Phelan guessed that he was continuing the discussions he must have engaged in at Parisian sidewalk cafes as a student, nursing a Pernod, and advocating the overthrow of French colonialists in Syria.

Phelan was reassured. He understood Khahil's pitch: that they were both cultured men, conversing in the language of culture. If violence was the subject, it was nevertheless violence to be controlled by an élite capable of disciplining fellows such as the one who had tackled Phelan on the bridge. Phelan was diffident of élitist ideas but was in no doubt that he would rather be accepted by the élite than be flayed on the feet.

"Intelligence without passions remains abstract," Khahil was saying, and Phelan noticed how restless his hands had become, "but passions get nowhere without intelligence. It would be an enormous satisfaction for that fellow who tackled you on the bridge if I threw you into prison. But when he finishes his duty, ours begins. He cannot understand that, he cannot see the revolution as a whole. His kind are bricks in a building which will be completed only in the future. A study of history, Monsieur Phelan, makes you admit that you cannot make bricks without straw."

"I'm not really a student of history, Captain," said Phelan "but I do know we've given up making bricks with straw."

"The revolution cannot proceed without sacrifices, Monsieur Phelan," said Khahil rapidly. "A people can be galvanized by struggle and a vision. But some cannot grasp the vision, some must fall in the struggle. There are others to replace them. People are expendable: it's something you don't like to admit in the coddled, bourgeois West. Is there anything else?"

Khahil had become more emphatic and a little flustered. But apparently the re-education session was over, for as he concluded he rose, restored Phelan's passport and emptied camera and accompanied him to the door.

Phelan restrained himself from breaking into a run as he descended the stairs. Street lights were on, but he saw with surprise that the fellow who had captured him was still standing by the exit. Hands tucked into the pockets of his leather jacket, he stared morosely at Phelan, who would have liked to have chanced a flippant "salaam" but thought the better of it. He feared a bullet in the back, or at least, a roughing-up, but he was allowed to walk off. He wandered through the city streets, as he did not want to ask anyone for directions, until he found his airline office and advanced his booking to the first flight available, which was the following morning, even though it meant going to Istanbul rather than Beirut as he had intended. He bought the local French-language paper to while away the night, then headed for his hotel.

He was tense with the thought that his room had been ransacked, but he found nothing out of place. The Mosque of Omar tile still nestled at the bottom of his bag. After searching for a hiding place, he slipped it under the paper lining of the wardrobe. He would claim an earlier traveler must have left it there, if they developed his film with its shots of Israel and came for him. That was his nagging fear. Khahil might have plotted all along to take him during the night, or, even if he were not so diabolical, he might want to put him through a real interrogation once the film was developed.

Phelan tested the lock on the door several times. It was not even normally firm but, in any case, it would have been no protection. He did not put on his pyjamas for the half-admitted reason that they would enable his circumcision to be seen more easily. He read the thin French-language daily a few times, tried to placate his anxiety-hunger with a bar of chocolate, then stood at the window watching the dominant neon sign on the hillside opposite and wondering whether it should be translated "Long Live the Socialist Revolution" or "Long Live Revolutionary Socialism." He tried to convince himself it was a distinction with a difference. Until now he had considered himself mildly leftist.

He attempted ineffectually to rest on the bed with his eyes closed, then opened *The Mandelbaum Gate,* which he had finished on the trip. After a few minutes he threw it aside for, although he admired it, in these circumstances its agile artifice irritated him. He stood at the window watching the neon hymn to revolutionary socialism fade like a bad dream with the advance of dawn. It was the last thing he remembered before he was awoken by stormtroopers banging at the door. The lock and key were dancing. Phelan sat up in his unspoiled bed in confused terror at the Arabic shouting. His head throbbed and he saw before him the implacable Khahil. Then the shouting, which was also in execrable French, began to unscramble.

"Hurry: car late for airport. Monsieur overslept? Monsieur sick?"

"I'm dressed and packed," answered Phelan. "Won't keep you waiting a jiffy."

He was deliriously happy in the car, which called at a house to pick up two of the plane crew. They invited Phelan in and, although he usualy avoided it, he drank with pleasure the concentrated black coffee they offered.

"Do you like this regime?" he asked provocatively. "It could be worse," one pilot answered sardonically "...I think."

Phelan had to restrain himself from singing as the car made toward the airport. Daybreak seemed arrested as leaden clouds hung on the horizon. Frequently the car was forced off the road by cumbersome, dun green tanks which rolled in a long line toward the capital.

The last trap, Phelan mused, would be the airport: a soft-voiced official who would take him by the arm just as he was to submit to passport control and ask him to clear up a few details in a nearby cubicle. But he was convinced that he was out of the B-grade movie by now, that the fellow on the bridge was merely an excitable busybody and Captain Khahil a polite official who enjoyed reviving the theories of his schooldays. Phelan accused himself of an overheated imagination once he was involved and could not maintain a reportorial detachment. He regretted leaving the Mosque of Omar tile in the hotel wardrobe.

"And so we say farewell to Damascus, city of Oriental mystery and revolutionary socialism," he Fitzpatricked to himself as the Caravelle gained height, "where the setting sun of Sorel throws its dusky pink fingers on the crescent moon of Islam." The hostess passed with the morning papers. Phelan chose the only non-Arabic one, the French-language daily.

Captain Khahil was staring at him from the front page. He had been shot by a fanatic as he left his office last evening. Four bullets had hit him as he descended the steps. The killer, whose photograph did not appear, would be hanged today.

Phelan, exhausted, dozed on the flight to Istanbul, but woke several times to reread the item. He saw red on blue, Captain Khahil spurting blood to stain his spotless uniform. Even though the killer's photograph did not appear, Phelan was sure he knew the laurel-wreathed face of this poet of the revolution.

As he had to wait for a connection in Istanbul, Phelan decided to stay overnight and catch up on lost sleep. Despite the low ceiling of rain-laden clouds which made the Bosphorous gray, he enjoyed Istanbul. After Damascus, it was shabby, large and relaxed. The cars were mainly old, outsize American monsters; people fished from the wharves and cooked their gleaming catch on charcoal fires; there were ferry rides. He felt at home as in his Sydney. Wandering along the waterfront, he came to a statue of Ataturk, which reminded him that here, too, there had been a revolution forty years ago. But Istanbul, rather Constantinople, had survived. He resolved to return to Damascus and photograph the witch's hat minarets for his grandchildren in the first years of the third millenium.

The short stories of Desmond O'Grady, Rome correspondent for the Melbourne Age *and the* Sydney Morning Herald, *are published in prestigious journals in Australia, the USA, England and the Philippines. He is equally adept with humorous and serious material. Mr. O'Grady's story "Yours Sincerly" (no spelling error) appeared in SSI No. 36.*

"I used to think of her as the Hsi Shih
of Suh Gung Lee Baan—a Cinderella who could
have bewitched an emperor..."

Mrs. CMS

BY JACK REYNOLDS

ONE sunny Saturday afternoon in the summer of 1949—only a few months before the Commies came—we *wy gwaw run* or foreigners were leading a healthy open-air life on the hostel veranda when Chang Ming Sang approached and asked us if we would honor him by attending a performance that night at the theater he had recently opened at Law Jiah Bah, a village two-thirds of the way down to the river.

"Will your wife be performing?" I asked.

"She is the star."

"Then I, for one, will be there."

"Me too," said Mike, and "Me too," said Pete, for we were all great admirers of the lady we called, from her husband's initials, Mrs. CMS.

Accordingly, at a quarter past seven that evening, Peter, Mike and I added shirts and shoes to our shorts and set off. As we walked through Suh Gung Lee we found an unusual number of the inhabitants going our way, and when, about a minute later, we walked round the hairpin bend onto the brink of the Yangtze valley, and looked down over the knotted mountain ranges and the glimmering ricefields to the smudge of yellow haze which overhung the river, we could see that all the lines of the declining road and hilltops, every winding path with its load of stragglers in single file, was running down to meet and culminate in the theater at Law Jiah Bah. Chang Ming Sang's theater, that breathless Saturday night, was the hub of the universe.

In the gathering dust, we made our way towards the entrance. Queues are unheard of in China, at least since the pigtail went out of fashion, and it was like throwing yourself into a king-size rugger scrum. But, waving aloft our complimentary tickets, we sailed past the barricades—to be promptly knocked backwards by the unbelievable stench which always knocks you backwards just inside a Chinese theater. (There is no Gents, let alone a Ladies; people who are caught short just walk to the nearest wall and let go.)

This theater in Law Jiah Bah resembled that in London's Regent's Park in just one particular: it also was open-air. There the resemblance ended. For the Law Jiah Bah theater was in fact a disused truckyard. On one side were the backs of the teashops which lined the street. On the other, behind a fence of groggy palings, was a 100-foot-high cliff, on which a large throng of non-paying spectators had already assembled, very precariously, and in every stage of deshabille down to the complete nudity of several infants. "Where else in the world," I asked Mike, "do women attend the theater in their underwear?" (This was twenty years before the Woodstock festival, when a lot of the audience wore nothing at all. Such audience-participation was beyond our innocent imagining in the late 1940's.)

No sumptuously upholstered seats received us, but rows of narrow benches placed on each side of narrow tables. If you sat on a bench on the stageward side of the table, you had something to lean against while you watched the show, but you had to turn round every time you wanted a sip of tea. If you sat behind the table you could get at your teacup without making a corkscrew of yourself, but you had nothing to lean against. You couldn't even lean on the table, for there was no room for your teacup (sunk in a hole, like an inkwell in a school desk), your dried sunflower and watermelon seeds, half a dozen babies, three or four piles of airing nappies, *and* your elbows. Indeed, there was scarcely room for you in the theater at all.

Numbers had been painted on the tables, and one person was supposed to sit at each number. But no allowance had been made for the extra fat man in the middle, or for the lady who had brought in half a dozen sucklings on one ticket, and was to spend the entire performance feeding them, one after another, from apparently inexhaustible founts. However, the seats had cost only 200,000 CNC, then equivalent to 1.25 American cents; you got your tea thrown in, and what Chinese ever worried about comfort? To our neighbors, this was an unusually well-appointed place of entertainment.

All eyes were fixed on the curtains as though everybody expected them to rise on time. Nothing, of course, was more unlikely. Stretched across the curtains was a pink silk banner on which the name of our Unit was inscribed in ornate Chinese characters. Smaller characters announced that we were honoring the theater with our presence that night, and that it was the hope of the management that we would not find the show disappointing. I was touched. Not thus, I told myself, had Lilian Bayliss greeted my presence in the gods at Sadler's Wells (sixpence early doors, ninepence if you came late) though I'd seldom missed a Saturday night performance in pre-war days for years, except when prior speedway commitments had kept me away in summertime...

Suddenly Chang Ming Sang appeared beside us, his teeth shining in that especially formal but expansive smile which he reserved for occasions when he was host. He was one of our most dashing drivers and his private life seemed to have been as full of dash as his professional one. For any man could come as a penniless refugee from distant Anhuei province and fall in love with a famous actress from Chungking. Such a man seldom gets beyond applauding extra heartily from the front row of the gallery. But Chang Ming Sang had got himself a job in the theater. He had made himself known to the actress. She was a lovely creature, the adopted daughter of the manager, who had bought her for five silver dollars on a small-town street and kicked and beaten her through her teens to stardom. Chang Ming Sang had talked to this vision of loveliness in that polite, persuasive, persistent way of his, every sentence ending with an "ah," either sharp, or enquiring, or tender, or jocular, or harsh. There was an amazing subtlety and variety in the range of Chang Ming Sang's "ah's;" I have heard them charm us out of tight spots with rapacious customs officials, marauding Kuomintang soldiery, murderous bandits, and the most lethal tribesmen on the Tibetan border, the Nosu (or the Lolo, as the Chinese called them). Nobody could withstand such eloquence, coupled with such a dulcet delivery.

Certainly the actress couldn't. She eloped with him—thus plunging the manager and his family into bankruptcy and ruin. The lovers fled to Kweiyang, where eventually Chang Ming Sang had become one of our drivers.

For three years (I was told) they remained in love with each other. This was an all-time record for China, where I was once told that "no one can be in love for more than a week. After that she's just your wife and you're just her husband." Gradually, therefore, Mrs. CMS began to pine for the drums and violins, the thunder of applause when as many as three people forget themselves and begin to clap all together, as sometimes happens in a Chinese theater. She even recalled with regret her adopted father. He had kicked and beaten her, it was true, but also he had made her a celebrity. And she had repaid him by ruining him... About this time her father found out where she was, and went to Kweiyang to plead with her to return to him. Shortly after, Mrs. CMS resumed her theatrical career.

Mrs. CMS had a grace of carriage not often attained by Chinese women on the mainland. With her dark brown skin, her strangely sleepy eyes, her large un-Chinese mouth, she looked more like a Balinese woman than like a daughter of Han. There was no telling which part of the country she had come from. Her parents had been refugees. They had gladly sold her while she was still small. She could barely remember them.

She could do anything a mortal ever did on a one-wheel cycle. She could walk the tightrope, do cartwheels and the splits, strike ballerina poses while standing on various portions of another girl's anatomy. She could sing love songs, heroic songs and bawdy comic songs; and she danced with so much grace that she made all the other girls look like embarassed elephants. In addition, she was an inexhaustible mine of farcical plots and situations and she could well have been one of the world's leading comedy dramatists if only she had been able to write. Withal she was a good-hearted woman, who looked after her husband, her children, herself, and quite a crowd of hangers-on. I used to think of her as the Hsi Shih of Suh Gung Lee Baan—a Cinderella who could have bewitched an emperor, and caused him to ruin himself and his dynasty for her sake. But there were no emperors left to be bewitched. Instead, she was now readying her troupe backstage...

Chang Ming Sang asked us if we were comfortable—"of course, of course"—and, at our request, outlined the finances of the enterprise. This was the fourth night the theater had been operating. It gave one show a night, at eight. (How blandly he told us this, with his wristwatch pointing to 8:25!) The previous night they had grossed 34,000,000 CNC. Twenty percent of the takings had to be paid, immediately after the show each night, to the village headman and a few other dignitaries, in return for which the headman guaranteed protection if anything happened. It cost 14,000,000 CNC every day to feed the cast and staff. That left about 13,000,000 for expenses such as costumes, lights, rent, and tea for the customers.

By nine o'clock, we had given up hope that anything would happen that night and were wondering how much longer we must wait before we could withdraw without discourtesy. This is the point you always reach sooner or later in a Chinese theater, the point of exasperation; but just as you start to leave your seat, the curtain goes up, and you have to sit down again, looking foolish. This process is known in military parlance as "softening up" the enemy: the management cleverly gets you so bored with *nothing* that you will be pleased with just about *anything*.

Suddenly, without warning, the curtain jerked up and revealed to us four ladies of various shapes, sizes and ages going through something like—but not very like—an old-time Goldwyn girl routine. They were dancing without any musical accompaniment, and seemed to have started the dance long before the curtain went up; as though their part of the bargain was just to dance, and it was up to the stage manager to raise the curtain if and when he felt like it. The girls continued to hop and skip in a silence broken only by a hoarse voice calling to the trumpeter that the show was on and it was time for him to play. Suddenly he gave an almighty blast, throwing all the girls out of gear, but they quickly recovered themselves; and slowly it dawned on us that the tune was familiar—that popular number from our Sunday school days: *"Shall we gather at the river?"*

The one on the extreme left, I was explaining to Peter, is Mrs. CMS's brother's wife, the one who always gets the black eyes; and the bold and beefy hussy next to her is his other wife, the one who hands out the said black eyes. The gorgeous animal next to her, I told Peter, you will recognize as Mrs. CMS's sister, another five dollar waif "adopted" by the impressario. Finally, the one on the far right, with the lovely tawny skin and the sleepy eyes...

"I know, I know," Peter said. "It's Mrs. CMS herself."

Then, again without warning, and to the obvious surprise of the dancers, who hadn't nearly finished yet, the curtain fell and the trumpet gave up in the middle of a particularly flat note. Everybody had a sip of tea and picked up a fresh handful of sunflower seeds to nibble at. These they shelled in the usual Chinese "no hands" manner, using teeth and tongue only, and spitting the detritus in all directions.

I never have been able to understand why there are such long intervals in a Chinese vaudeville theater. Obviously there is feverish activity behind the lowered curtain. Men are rushing about, shouting at each other, dragging heavy objects across the boards; the curtains are bellied about by many a miniature tornado caused by human beings in rapid motion; elbows and bottoms momentarily mold them to strange contours; a wildly agitated face is occasionally thrust between them to gaze briefly in depair at the audience, then whipped back suddenly. And what is the final result? The curtain goes up on exactly the same scene as before—an empty stage and the same old backdrop...

Programs at Chang Ming Sang's theaters were always divided into three parts. First came Les Girls, dancing and singing as a troupe, in solos, in duets, in trios, and in a variety of fetching costumes. (Mrs. CMS, that amazing woman, made all the costumes too.) After Les Girls came the Drama. Finally, as climax, we would be given the Thrills—the tightrope or trick cycling or conjuring tricks.

That evening, as I remember, the drama was one of Mrs. CMS's slighter efforts. It concerned an orphan girl who, having no parents to arrange things for her, had to ask the public notary to help her find a husband. The first scene was full of comedy, with the girl quite desperate for a husband but struggling to act like a lady of refinement, and the notary, sizing her up as he ground his ink, continually hinting that a well-oiled palm can achieve much more than a dry one. Finally, when he had bled her as much as he deemed politic, he hitched up his sleeves and wrote the "Husband Wanted" ad...

Two prospective bridegrooms apply. One is an impecunious scholar who is interested only if the girl has money, the other a ne'er-do-well and fop. Each makes a good impression at first but later makes a false move and is rejected. They decide to revenge themselves on the girl for their disappointment. They find a dirty and uncouth coolie who is selling flowers, dress him up in fine clothes and give him a few quick lessons in etiquette: "A gentleman never sits on a stool when talking to a lady; he sits on the table smoking a cigarette and swinging his leg." When this impostor is presented, the girl, dazzled by his good looks, his fine clothes, his elegant manners—He studied in America, that's why he acts so strange—falls in love with him at once, marries him and takes him home.

The last scene occurs at their home immediately after the wedding. The girl wants to buy some flowers to decorate the bedroom and is surprised to find the bridegroom so knowledgeable about which varieties are in bloom. She goes out while the fop, the scholar and the notary congratulate the bridegroom on his success, point out that he owes it all to them, and try to extract some of his newly won fortune from him. While they are still importuning him, the wife returns and starts to arrange the flowers in an old rice-wine bottle.

"How much did you give for those flowers?" asks her husband. She tells him and he howls with anger.

"You've been rooked," he shouts. "Yesterday I was selling them on the street for half that price."

The curtain falls, as it so often falls in Mrs. CMS's plays, on the spectacle of an incensed wife belaboring her husband and his men friends with a *tiao* or wooden shoulder-pole. And the audience roars with laughter because it has all been so true to life but so much funnier than real life seems to be.

By now complete darkness had fallen. The glow of the footlights was flung upwards into the night. It covered the theater like a tent of transparent gold, through which the stars stared down, on another non-paying audience. The heat was still stifling. Everywhere fans were wagging back and forth. In the reflected light from the stage, the cliff on our right now looked like a choir of angels, for almost everyone was in white, the men in singlets and long white trousers, the women in scant white undervests worn outside their brief white hot-weather *shiao koo dzuh*.

The *kie-shway* or hot water man had put away the long-spouted watering can with which he had been regularly topping up our teacups since the show began; he was now collecting the cups in a wicker basket. The woman in front of me turned round for a final swig before surrendering her cup. The baby at her breast refused to surrender his. She joggled him up and down to stop his guzzling. She caught my eye and smiled. "Is the show enjoyable, Big Beard?" she asked. "The best part comes now."

The curtain had already gone up, the left side more reluctantly than the right, as usual. A small girl was flying round and round the stage on a one-wheel cycle. She was a skinny little kid, the daughter of Mrs. CMS's brother by his larger wife. She had none of the charm of Mrs. CMS's own small daughters, Little Chicken and Little Flower. She continued to circle the stage at great speed and with a deadpan expression on her face until a shout from the wings told her to stop. She went off and Mrs. CMS pedaled on.

Mrs. CMS was transformed. She was attired in a loose white silk blouse and shorts which fitted her like a glove. She circled the stage two or three times, the blouse rippling as she rushed through the air, her long wavy black hair streaming behind her. Gone was her usual sleepy expression. Her eyes were sparkling. Her face was flushed and happy.

It is impossible to describe all the feats she performed on that shiny one-wheeler. But the last, of course, was the best. Somebody handed her an air-rifle and then stood at the edge of the stage, right, holding a small gong at arm's length. Mrs. CMS described tight circles at furious speed, left. She loaded the rifle as she rode, put it to her shoulder, took aim at the gong. The first time she missed and laughed aloud. Again she loaded the gun while in full careen, again took aim while flying round and round in tiny circles. This time she found the mark. The gong swung violently as the pellet hit it. A musical chime floated out over the theater.

Mrs. CMS leapt off her machine and with bike in one hand, rifle in the other, bowed to us all. The great mane of hair came tumbling over her head and fell before her, almost sweeping the floor. She flung it back and marched off, springy and slim, a gallant figure.

Almost immediately she was back again. This time she had an apparently normal machine with two wheels. But when she stood in the middle of the stage and swung it round and round herself with one hand on the saddle she could make the handlebars and front wheel rotate like a top. Then she vaulted into the saddle, facing front. She did one lap of the fifteen-foot square stage in that conventional posture. Then for the next five minutes she rode that bike in every conceivable manner except the orthodox one. Sitting backwards on the handlebars and pedaling with her feet. Lying with her stomach on the saddle and pedaling with her hands. Riding on the back wheel only with the front one reared up a yard above the ground. Riding with her shoulders on the saddle and her body hairpinned, steering with her feet. Riding with her chest on the saddle and her body hairpinned backwards, again steering with the feet. Finally standing on her head on the saddle, with her legs straight up and V'd, pedaling with each hand in turn as a pedal came up within reach...

The exertions had brought the silk blouse adrift from its moorings and it fell to her armpits. She somersaulted off the bike and caught it with one hand as it came towards her. Quickly she tucked the blouse back inside her shorts, blushing and laughing. She was vestless and braless. Peter was applauding vigorously.

Her brother's two wives, now dressed in ordinary blue split-sided gowns, with brown stockings flopping over the garters just above their knees in approved high society style, appeared on stage, each bearing three ordinary restaurant stools. Each stacked her three benches in a pile, one on top of the other, tested the rigidity of the pile, then squatted beside it to hold it steady. The two piles were at right angles to each other and a bike's length apart.

Mrs. CMS had now got her breath back, and her costume in order. She too checked the piles of stools, then, satisfied, lifted the bike on them, with one wheel on each pile. Climbing up the stools she stepped carefully onto the precariously balanced bike, standing with her left foot on the left pedal. The front wheel, which she held at right angles to the back one, ran agitatedly along its stool top, a few inches each way, until she was set; if it had gone a whole foot one way or the other, she would have come crashing down, bike, stools and all. Slowly she lowered herself to a squatting position on the pedal, with both hands on the handle bars, and the front wheel jerking backwards and forwards along the top of its stool as her balance shifted. At last she was set: with a lightning movement she snatched her right hand from the handlebars, thrust it under the crossbar, and gripped the rim of the front wheel with it. Then she began to thrust her head under the crossbar. It was an awful struggle, a struggle which held all watchers breathless. The smaller wife had dropped her head on the thin arms with which she was holding the front pile of stools steady. It looked as if she was praying that the trick would succeed.

At last Mrs. CMS got her head under the bar, through to the right side of the machine. She now had to get her left hand through while holding the bike steady with her right hand on the front wheel. This was a crucial moment. Cautiously the left hand came off the handlebars, was eeled through the frame, and reached blindly up for the handlebars again. The hand groped and jerked foolishly. People began to laugh, but there was anxiety in their laughter. The front wheel moved dangerously far to one side and back again. Suddenly the hand caught on what it sought. It was easier now. Mrs. CMS slid the rest of her body through the frame. One leg arrived, and was placed on the right pedal. At last the other leg was pulled through to the right side of the machine, and she struck a triumphant pose, standing on the leaning bike with one foot on the pedal and one hand on the handlebars on the opposite side of the machine from which she had started.

There was a slight spatter of clapping which in China amounted to an ovation. But she hadn't finished yet. Carefully she lowered herself to a squatting position on one pedal, the other one this time, and began to repeat the trick backwards. You could see her breast heaving from the exertion. She had an even fiercer struggle to get her head under the crossbar this time. The gropings of her hand were more prolonged and even more frantic. The bike wobbled so violently that she once came within an inch of disaster. The hand was raised jerkily again and again. But at last it snatched what it was seeking. With a sinuous movement she snaked the rest of her body through the frame and struck that Eros pose again, back where she started.

"That is all for tonight, please come again," she cried, then she leapt lightly to the stage, catching the bike as it fell.

The show was over. We rose from our benches and made for the narrow wicket. For a few minutes we were firmly wedged in by a mass of struggling, sweating bodies, unable to pry our limbs free, borne along by the gigantic forces of China. Then we were outside and standing on our own feet again. A rickshaw man like a bandit importuned us. A few late peddlers were folding up their stalls. Across the road, a man was waving a flaming piece of paper outside his front door, to scare the devils away from his house for the night.

Jack Reynolds, who led a swashbuckling life, is best known as a writer. This story is based on his experience while West China Director and Transport Manager for the Friends' Ambulance Unit, just prior to and after the Communist take-over. He was originally introduced in SSI No. 5 with his short story "The Old Shoe." Mr. Reynolds presently lives in Bangkok with his Thai wife and seven children.

"And yet not one of them advanced
his acquaintance with him far enough to
become a true friend..."

An Empty Bed

BY YEHIA HAKKI

IF you turn out of the Imamein Square into El Rihan Street, and take
only a few steps forward, you will come, on your left hand side, to a
small shop which you will not notice as you walk past, for it is one of a
close-set indistinguishable row of shabby shops, marching exactly
in step with the narrow, dilapidated pavement, in every one of its
twists and turns, and every one of its straight runs. This shop and its
companions are enveloped in a tattered web of murkiness, woven by
a spider long-since dead, and since lodged in, first by confidence and
prosperity, then by sloth and by hard times. The springs that set the
puppets in motion behind the shop-fronts have grown rusty. A head
hangs down upon a breast. A pair of eyelids move like cumbersome
door-bolts, pulled upwards by cords and then falling heavily back
into place. A hand trembles as it shunts from the task of receiving
small coinage to the task of handing over a customer's purchase,
and then to driving away the flies which are trying to drink their fill of

the saliva that dribbles down between the lips, and the rheum at the corner of an eyelid, and the ropy fluid with the attractive glossy color, which oozes out of the channel of an ear.

If you raise your eyes slightly as you walk past this particular shop, and you catch sight of the signboard above it, it will dispirit you: you will avert your glance and hurry onward—even if you are someone who can walk in scarcely anything more than a decrepit shuffle. Worried, you will exclaim to yourself, "This cursed employment, squeezing itself in among shops that are carrying on the sort of decent trades that are praised in the Holy Book and praised by the Prophet, shops whose owners you wouldn't hesitate to shake hands with and sit down with to a meal. It's all wrong that this shop should be here: a pimple on a smooth cheek, a whore among chaste women, a leper in the harem of an oriental potentate—one who, as though his mere presence were not bad enough, gets drunk on fresh milk handed to him by a noble-blooded pimp."

Luckily for you, your fit of depression will be driven away by your pride in your own powers of deduction; you will think yourself the first passer-by sharp enough to have noticed that the signboard must originally have hung over another shop that was broader in its frontage, for it juts out left and right over the two neighboring shop-fronts—a comparatively modest form of encroachment upon them on its part, for its shadow covers the whole stretch of ground below. Leaning forward slightly, and with a very pronounced list to one side, the signboard might be on the verge of tumbling down; and yet it has hung there throughout the years.

The shop to the right is a small grocery store that supplies local produce. Just inside is a dusty counter of blistered wood on which you can see some pickled aubergines; everyone of them has overripe seeds spilling out of its guts, while the decomposed flesh of the vegetable is falling apart in shreds, making the mouth of a customer water if he is of the vulture or of the hyena kind.

The shop on the left belongs to a leather-worker who makes bags, a craftsman in the left-overs of the butcher's trade, for the lid on one bag is the flank of a cow, the body of the next is the belly of a goat—suitcases made for separations, bags to hasten departures; strewn over railway platforms, squeezed into luggage racks, they roam the earth like homeless souls.

A donkey cart lumbers past, giving off a faint odor of toddy; a chicken coop without a roof or sides, crammed with black-garbed women, everyone of them brooding upon her egg—and God help her if it does not hatch out, for they are, everyone, involved in a race against a thieving kite, forever voracious, ever hovering patiently to swoop down upon their chicks. The donkey that draws the cart is bony and underfed; you can tell that the driver, although he is short of wind, is an insatiably avaricious person.

You glance back at the signboard once more before it passes out of your sight, at the sprawling, ornate letters of its inscription, daubed on in white paint which is full of cracks that give it a tortoise-shell pattern: UNDERTAKER FOR WHOLE OF IMAMEIN DISTRICT.

The master-undertaker's apprentice leaves the shop entrance for the inner depths, a dark cave inside which the glances of a passer-by dissolve in thin air: he returns carrying on his shoulder a brand-new coffin together with its wrapping cloth, and hangs them both up on a nail upon one flap of the shop-door. Then he sits down, and polishes his nails by rubbing them against his striped garment.

Opposite the shop there have lived for a long time a small family: the father, the mother, and their only son—for the firstborn had also been the last. The neighbors do not know much about them. They realize that the family wish to lead a retired life and believe that people who withdraw in that way want to conceal very great happiness, or else very deep grief, either of which is a mortifying stigma for any unobtrusive person to live with. Those who say that there is happiness behind the veil of privacy claim that you can sense this; in any case, they add, it is plain to your own eyes when it bursts into view on saints' days and at feasts, for on those occasions there stream down from the windows of that home a festive blaze of lights and a reverberating laughter that have no equal in the entire quarter. Those who hold that there is unhappiness behind the screen of privacy point to an event that recurs once or twice a month. There draws up at the door an old car battered in body and spirit, with the air of a pregnant woman whose child has been smothered to death in her womb: a mother who gives birth to death, where others produce new life. Out of the car steps a huge-bodied attendant, in charge of a tall thin man with a sallow face, a shifty glance, and hair in wild disorder. He is always slily on the look-out for the moment when he can regain his freedom, and fly off in pursuit of an enemy who has destroyed his spirit, his consciousness and his reasoning powers, and left him a flair for using language as disgusting as a piece of chewed sugar-cane which has been spat out—words that he masticates with relish as his peculiar form of self-expression. The trouble is that he does not know who that enemy is. He grips hold of the car-door, then of the front door of the house; the attendant hauls him away, and with the palms of his hands, sets the man's face looking forwards so that he shall not twist his neck, and so that passers-by might be protected from the looks which he shoots at them like bullets and the foul language which would disgrace the most disreputable brothel.

When this outcry starts up, all the windows in the house slam shut at one and the same instant, as though they did so automatically and without anyone touching them. An hour or two later, the attendant emerges, still chewing the remains of a meal, wiping his moustache with one hand, his other hand held tight by the gentle, tender clasp of a tall emaciated child with a gentle soft look, who takes his seat in the car, and gives a quiet little gasp, as though he has just come back from a long ride on a lame horse and has found his own familiar bed waiting for him.

Those who maintain that the family has a secret grief assert with a discoverer's exultation and with the triumph of a gambler who has won a bet, that this is the man of distinction whom the family has produced, a man whose great fortune alone prevents them from praying earnestly for his death, since our religious law does not allow a killer to inherit the wealth of his victim, even if he kills him out of mercy for him.

It often happens that after the car moves off, the bottle-washer comes out of the cafe carrying a pail brimfull of slops out of the hubble-bubbles. He stands on the pavement and empties his pail in one powerful sweep, and the earth feels a delightful tingle, as the water splatters down upon its skin while the aroma of the dottle spreads out like an opiate soothing the nerves of all creatures who are passing by—men, horses, mules, and donkeys alike.

The truth is simpler than any of the surmises which have been made. The veil of secrecy had been drawn, not to hide any happiness or grief, but for another purpose, which has never been uncovered in spite of all the ingenious guesswork, and because it is more plausible, and truer to human nature—for deception plays with illusions and not with the truth, and makes fancied things shine brightly so as to dim realities. The family have chosen the only observance which requires a screen to be drawn round it if its rites are not to be disturbed and their effects nullified. They have broken with the world of men. To them it is a hornets' nest which you must keep clear of, a landmine which does you no harm so long as you merely walk around it, but which you must never touch, a sealed wineskin with the promise of a deliciously intoxicating bouquet, which when you break it open, transforms itself, and your mind with it, into floating vapors of lightheadedness. For them, life is not a vertical progress in which the new builds itself up upon the old and from which you can view an ever-widening horizon as you climb upwards. Neither is it the circling orbit of a planet, rising, climbing to its zenith, sinking, and then setting. It is, instead, a faint horizontal line, made up of a myriad of identical dark spots, soldered together so thoroughly that you can no longer make out any color in them. Even their food is chewed for them in advance by mincing-machines and pestles: they eat meat and vegetables all pounded into one soggy mash; what they relish is the way that every ingredient loses its distinctive flavor. Opting out of life was their way of escape from direct confrontation with the most powerful and unconditional form of a grace, to which they would otherwise have had to bow down their heads as low as the earth and never raise their foreheads. This would have been a wearisome posture, and weariness is the broadest of the gates through which faithlessness finds its way in. In their rejection of a professed blessing, they acknowledge its value more so than others; they are far more conscious of an obligation which should be owed in return.

They had disengaged themselves because of a fear of receiving, as a recompense, something in whose aridity they might drown, or in whose floodwaters they might be sucked dry. They were trying to ensure in this way that they would be free from mental distress, safe from regrets at the monstrous faithlessness of others, or from grief at the baseness which they would discover in their own personalities if they ever stood in abject fear of the lassitude which lay in wait for them, and which would pin them down in terror as a snake does a sparrow. For you may stake your life upon your always remaining a stingy cowardly creature, but you dare not venture so much as a farthing upon your remaining—always and in all circumstances— courageous and generous. Having withdrawn from others, they no longer distinguish one day from another by name: they tell the passing of the days by the way in which the shadows, cast by familiar objects, gradually circle round in an arc, by identifying the calls of migrant birds: for those who cut themselves off from the world of men draw closer to nature. As the days have become confused, so have their ages; the husband calls his wife "Mother," she calls him "Father;" both of them call their only son "My friend," while he calls his mother "Darling." He has no word at all for his father, since he stopped addressing him when he was five years old; he never speaks *to* him, never speaks *of* him in his presence, and if he is not there, he uses the plain personal pronoun, the mere monosyllable "Him."

Often, if they both turned their backs upon each other, while one of them was leaving the room, the father would look behind him and find that the son was staring back at him. The son would feel that his father was giving him a piercing look which foreboded something. The father would feel that his son's glance was the look of a person with a gleaming scalpel hidden in his hand. Then the interchanged looks would turn into the embarassed, apologetic smiles of men whose ruses have been detected; then the smiles, in their turn would change into two looks of understanding, love and esteem: the whole incident would take only a brief moment—and revealed that the family was close-knit, and shared a distinctive feature: every one of them was tender, soft, hypersensitive, as a result of having disengaged himself from others.

Life without a program. No wonder the parents showed no surprise, no objection, no regret, when the son broke off his studies at the Faculty of Commerce, after spending a year there which had started out for him with no anxieties or fixed dislikes, but left him with a burning hatred of money and of bookkeeping: whenever he swore now, he spat out a figure. They did not react any more strongly when he broke off his study of literature after devoting another year to that: he found that the standards of his mind and his language had been depraved, and that he was taking to a fatuous prattle. He followed this with a year spent idling at home: this fundamentally altered his life, for when it was over, he had altered his attitude. He found himself entering the Faculty of Law, and applied himself to his studies there, passing his examinations every year, though he was placed every time at the bottom of the list. His mind found rest in his studies there: he settled into them, and came within a year of graduation. He liked the way that the Law cut itself off so totally from the ordinances of nature, with their confusion, their contradictions, their claim that injustice was sometimes true justice in disguise, their lack of any final settlement—or, at the most, their postponing of it until the whole world lay in ruins. The Law has invented for itself a self-supporting logic which looks beautiful on paper, distinguished by ingenious subdivisions and sequences, and swift to take effect; as though it has demolished the structure of life, and has turned the rubble into numbered and catalogued matrixes with which it has built its own stronghold. A judge does not pronounce judgment by drawing upon his knowledge of truth—he relies upon paper—for *Paper* is clearer than *Truth*. A judge will reject any truth, as easily as a lie, unless it is supported by juridically-admissible evidence which has not been shown to be spurious. He gives vice clearly-defined limits; while virtue becomes a vague notion which is not taken into account at all: the judge imposes his penalty upon the adulterous husband, but does not grant a reward to a husband who remains faithful to his wife after their honeymoon is over.

With all this, the virtue of the law is that it relieves mankind by converting the world of the spirit into logical argumentation where there is no distinction between knowledge and ignorance, between freewill and the determined: it has dropped the word *fate* from the vocabulary of man, and in so doing it has at the same time dropped the word *pity*. No matter, for such is the logical sequence of arguments which the law follows; and however many injustices it may involve, a logical sequence of arguments is to be preferred to a just law which has no discernible logical structure. Forensic logic is so different from the logic of nature's ordinances, that little by little, the young man lost the sense of there being any distinction between virtue and vice. A beggar, who always receives and never gives, withdraws from the bustle of life, lies down on the pavement in front of a mosque, and lays his chest bare; he gives it up both to sunlight and to swarms of lice: and when the two streams that flow over his breast blend together, he finds a delight which makes him at one and the same time whimper with pain and quiver with pleasure.

During the period that the young man spent idling at home between his year as a student of literature and the beginning of his law studies, it was natural that one occupation should present itself as a cure for his torpor—an occupation which, of all others, is the simplest to enter upon, the easiest to continue in, the worthiest, the truest and most sensible—and that is the occupation of a husband. He was a virgin, but was determined that the woman he married should be one who was sexually experienced. He decided to make his choice without any intervention from his parents, to pick for himself the workshop that was going to yield up its products for him. He did not run through the list of his relations and neighbors and acquaintances, but seated in his own home, like a priest anointing an emperor, he stretched out his arm upon the head of a penniless girl, and he uttered the one brief phrase, "This one!" like a child in a toy shop. It filled him with boundless joy to think that he had returned to nature and her ways, and had trampled underfoot all the conventions which men had thought up for the winning of a wife: the pursuit, the cornering of the quarry, the carrying off of the prize, the deed of purchase, the hero's proving his prowess in battle, the courtship, the sleepless pillow and the sighings. Sometimes he smiled to himself because he had surmised by sheer mother-wit, without any direct knowledge of the matter, that the unrealized cause of the misery of modern woman is that she has inherited traits from every one of her ancestresses, and wishes her husband to win her by combining all these devices together and bringing them into play, although she falsely claims that because she is a civilized person, courting is the only method it is necessary to use. Why should he bother himself with all this palaver?

The penniless girl, together with her mother, used to come on visits with her father, who was a tenant on the land owned by the young man's family. They came to town whenever the half-yearly installments of their rent were due. For a dress, she still wore the old-fashioned *malas* of crinkly dyed silk; on her feet, instead of shoes, she wore slippers. She only revealed the tiniest portion of her face; in the grip of a crushing shyness, she would have buried herself in the ground if she could whenever anyone addressed her. He mentally added up her pink ankles and those parts of her face that he had managed to catch a glimpse of, and decided that it was she who would suit him. A simple, raw girl. Downcast eyes that dared not glance at you. A forehead free of any thought. A body in which the finer points of every part had been distributed in common throughout the whole. Matted hair which you could see would be bewitching once it was washed, and once it had been plaited so that it would hang upon her forehead and cheeks: he would rinse it for her with his own hands, and his tongue would find that the taste of soap could intoxicate as well as wine.

He knew that she had already been married to a relation of hers in their home village. The husband had had a rival who had a feud with him. Maliciously vindictive, he would not let him enjoy his newlywed bride in peace, but lay in wait for him when he was on his way home from the fields, and emptied bullets into him from a home-made rifle that he had bored for himself. A mangled corpse was carried home to the bride: she wiped the wounds with her handkerchief and in this way it became bloodstained for the second time in one week. To the young man, then, she was all that he could have hoped for: an easy path to take, already opened up and smoothed out for him by someone else. In the same way if he had bought an earthenware pot, turned and fired for use, he would have left it for someone else to dirty his fingers and scratch them in lining its inside with oil, so that he could use it for cooking. The girl was a better proposition than such a pot, because she was ready moistened—moist with blood, even if the outer layer of it came from the wounds of her murdered husband.

In order to complete his fancy, the young man set out to furnish the bridal-chamber which he had set aside for himself in his family home, in the style of a peasant of his wife's own class: a rush-mat at the edge of which slippers and wooden clogs were to be taken off and lined up; an iron bedstead with wooden planks stretched across it, and a mosquito-net of pink silk; a wooden chest to store clothes in, painted red and green, a basin and jug for washing. But when the bridal equipment was ready, he was taken by surprise to see her lips draw up and whisper in her mother's ear, after which she turned her face to the wall out of excess of shyness, keeping hold of her mother's hand and tugging at it, to make sure that she did not start saying anything while she was still in the room.

As soon as the young man was alone with his mother-in-law, she told him that what her daughter had whispered to her was, "As I'm marrying a Cairo man, and such a high-class man at that, I'd like to have at least a spring mattress on my bed instead of those planks of wood."

On that spring mattress the young man received the deepest shock of his life; it shook his being, and brought his illusions tottering down; it left him naked in the ruins, nursing the wounds of his bewilderment.

On the wedding night itself, the raw simple girl turned into a fierce wild beast, the downcast eyes gleamed like the eyes of a pouncing hawk, sending into the darkness of the night a glimmer like the flash of a sword or the sudden flaring-up of a smoldering fire; enough to set a brand ablaze, it was a thing that not the waters of all the sacred rivers flowing together could have quenched; it was a look that rasped his body like a file. The forehead that never gleamed with a single idea now had drawn upon it, in place of the smooth blankness of resignation, the execution order of a Court of Summary Justice that allowed no deferment and no appeal. The delicate, ever-closed lips opened and closed in audible smacks, and never kept the one shape for a single moment: at one instant, it was the circular brink of a volcano; the next, it was the inside of a funnelshaped vortex; next, a long slit like a dagger-wound; spasm succeeded spasm as though her gullet contained a grapnel which was being handled by a merciless grip. The open mouth revealed a set of teeth which gleamed with hunger, and dispelled the surrounding shadows by sending them scattering in alarm. The parts of her body which had pleaded that they had lost their individual attractions by having shared them out in common amongst them all, each retrieved its rights and in addition siezed and used as its own the enticements that are proper to a body as one single whole. Even her big toe reared itself up and tried to overreach itself. Her voracity was intensified by an underlying contradiction: the palms of her hands lay flat, resigned, passive, bestowing themselves, her arms were limp, the saliva of her mouth was cool and sweet as honey, and her breathing came like that of an innocent babe.

What was he to do? He came from a family which had never given anything of itself: he wanted a goblet of wine that he could swallow down in one gulp, not one that glued itself to his lips like a leech. He had sought his own pleasure, but before he could take it, he was caught in the grip of a liability. He could only accept a liability that he had undertaken of his own free will; he hated any obligation that was imposed upon him, like a poll-tax or a tribute—it was an invasion of the privacy behind which his self-respect preened itself. His self-respect, which was genuine enough, and true to itself, was a thing he was well satisfied with—so long as it remained insulated; he would allow no one else to scrutinize it; it was mortifying to be put in the balance, even if the opposite dish on the pair of scales contained no more than a mustard seed. If any uninvited hand claimed the right to weigh him, to test him, to assess him, then that hand ought to be lopped off.

In spite of his holding this view, he was too astonished to reach any decision. It was the raw simple girl who did so before he did. She bore with him for a second night; on the third, she gave him a kick and said, "We women from Upper Egypt were made for Upper Egyptian men. I piss on your money and your elegance and your fine words."

And she added, as though a prophetic voice spoke through her, "Find yourself a mummy all daubed with white and black and red: there's thousands of them in this town of yours."

She got up and gathered her few pieces of clothing together. In spite of his astonishment, the young man noticed for the first time the fine bridge of her nose, her long, slender neck, and a pair of firm haunches that the noblest Arab mare would have envied.

In the morning it was she who dragged her mother away by the hand, and glided out gingerly as though she were escaping from a captor who had fallen asleep and who might wake up at any moment; her crinkly *malas* of black silk hung forward, making her look as though she were preparing to run for it the moment she got past the door. And so her second marriage, also, lasted less than a week. When her mother caught a glistening in her eyes of what she took to be the vestiges of tears, she said to her, "Don't you grieve over him: God will send you better than that. This was your lot, and you had to go through with it."

And the daughter replied to herself, "You're so kind, mother, and such a fool! If I were to cry, it would be for my first husband all over again."

After that, the young man could satisfy his urges and heal his wound by visits to women who traded in passions; none of them had any rights over him and he had no liabilities towards any; he was happy to deal in cash purchases and not barter—a primitive method which time and progress have overlaid and buried. He made no distinction at first between any one of these women and another. But, after some time, he began to spruce himself up, and to search out the ones who attracted purchasers to their wares with the same draw that a lump of sugar has for a swarm of flies. The larger the swarm, and the more completely he was swallowed up in it, the more it pleased him: it made him feel that his face had become a mask. But he did not find the absolute pleasure he had hoped for: even with the ones in briskest demand, he thought he detected some turn of the head, some curl of the lip, some thrust of the arm, which upset his assurance. What he wished for now was a woman whose face would remain frozen in perfect stillness, even if it had to be made of wax, with lips rigid as wood, or fashioned in a mold, a woman who could not move her arms, even if that meant that she would be as cold as ice...and where should he find one like that?

No one can tell what would have become of him if he had not had a strange illness which kept him in bed for some time. The doctors said that it was a minor infection, a harmless microbe which is present even in the bodies of the fit, where the red corpuscles easily destroy it without artificial aid. His body, however, was unable to resist it, not because of any organic deficiency, but because he had lost his will to resist. Every medicine they gave him was so much lost effort: his physical frame became a field tussled over by the sweetness of life and the putrescence of decay.

It seemed animated by mere clockwork. He was like a breathing creature under whose skin every morsel of flesh had been eaten away by a gangrene, leaving nothing but the look that gleamed out of his eye-socket. The doctors recommended his father to consult a psychologist.

This piece of advice stung the young man to the quick. As soon as the doctors were out of the house, he got up, and went to the bathroom to draw the evil out of himself, and put the past behind him: he washed himself, purified himself, reaffirmed his faith. Freshened-up, his face, when he emerged, wore a look of content, of gentleness. His movements and gestures fell into a harmonious order, and grew unusually calm. As a result of this, in the days that immediately followed, some people looked upon him as dull-witted, although he thought of his mannerisms as the height of elegance, and now paid great attention to his fingernails and necktie, and saw to it that his clothes matched one another. He took to moving with a demureness which suggested a woman's coquettishness, to speaking in low, nasal tone; there was languor in his eyes; although his tall body now stooped slightly, this did not impair his good looks, but added a touch of deference, and, by setting off his head, even gave him, in some people's eyes, a deceptive air of acumen. In fact, to some, his stoop made him seem cunning and inquisitive—though God knows he was innocent of this.

And so that phase of his life came to a close. He entered the Faculty of Law, where his elegance and his sober bearing drew the notice of his fellow-students. They would hover around him, not knowing quite what attracted them to him: could it be his nails, his lithe fingers, the honey that flowed out of his eyes, or the curious quality in his voice? And yet not one of them advanced his acquaintance with him far enough to become a true friend, to be joined to him in an attachment which would separate them off from the crowd they were in. He did not feel lonely, but was quite at ease: to the honey of his looks he added a sweet-natured smile, which made him into a model of kindness and high-mindedness, in the eyes of the other students: "That," they would say to one another, "is how a really high-born young man behaves."

It was within a year of his final examinations. He lay on his bed one morning, and glanced out of his window. It was autumn. The Nile had fallen out of its summer stir and back into repose. It had been the liquor of zizyphus fruit coursing down from distant mountains: now it was a muddy browness as scaly as a fish's skin. Exhausted with its work of fecundating the earth, it withdrew into its burrow to hibernate; losing its prowess, it now suggested, more strongly than anything else could, the ague, the darkness of the lower depths, an enormous heaviness. The fields had put well behind them the days when they had been dry and naked, with a cracked skin; now they wore a mantle of blossoms, and offered its nectar to the bees and the grazing herds. A fresh breeze from a blue sky annihilated all malignancy. Lying on his bed, he could see the sky and watch a train of maiden clouds, brightly decked out and freshly combed, making fun of earth-dwellers by mimicking some of the things which can be seen in their lives. An unseen hand had poured out over the world a flood of happiness. A bird flew into view with a broad span of black wings, crying out as it bathed in the sunlight. It was a plover: the cry of that bird, according to his mother, presaged the arrival of a traveler. The bird's call only lasted a brief time, but in those moments were expelled from man all his chains and fetters, his captivity and fears, his uncertainties, delusions, and pollutions, and he became a pure and innocent being, who enjoyed a freedom that had no bounds, fit only for an angel or a fiend. This freedom floated down into the heart of the young man with a tremor. It vexed him that it should be so vigorous, and that it should not make itself fully plain to the limited vision of one who was a cross between angel and fiend. Well, then, he had no need of it. He turned his face to the wall. An appalling weariness seeped into him, and took over the whole of his being: it tinged his gullet with the bitterness of wormwood, it ran in his veins where his blood had run before; his body now sweated it out, his eyelashes were now spun out of it, and the dirt between his toes was now made of it.

He did not go out that day until later than his usual time. As he stepped out of his doorway, his eyes fell upon the small shop which stood opposite. It had lain empty for many months. Now, he saw that it had been opened up: a man upon a ladder was hanging up a board which read "Undertaker for Whole of Imamein District." His heart sank. Was it a mere chance that one and the same morning had brought him this world-weariness, and had seen the arrival of this servant of death? Could one of the two be the traveler whose arrival the plover had heralded? Or were events contrived according to some set plan, working out a prearranged purpose?

He saw the undertaker's apprentice—for that is what he took him to be—urging the workman on the ladder to hurry, with the result that the man misjudged the center of the rope as he was attaching it to its nail. As soon as the workman had come down off the ladder, the apprentice brought out a coffin and hung it up on one flap of the door. He felt that there was someone looking at him, and he looked up: the two glances met, and the appearance of the apprentice registered itself in the young man's mind in a clear-cut image, standing out from the rest of things, as though he were shining a spotlight onto him through some gaping hole in his own body. He saw a youngish man, with a body bulging like cotton in a hooped bale; stunted in height, with stumpy arms and bulky hands, a low forehead and narrow-slit eyes; his piercing look had the tinselly gleam of sequins, the whites of his eyes setting off a flame-colored glitter which spoke of cunning and rancor, of a disturbed and malicious spirit and the hunger of an animal: a creature determined to kill a rival with a glance would wear a look like this one. The young man was sure that he had seen this figure before. But where? He could not tell. Until he remembered that it had been in a book he had read about the theories of Darwin. His look, too; that was the look in his own father's eyes when the time had come for a sniff of cocaine or a shot of opium.

As he turned away, he saw that the apprentice was smiling at him, and raising his hand to his forehead in a friendly greeting. He walked away, knowing for certain that he would be coming back to him.

The friendship between them grew. The young man now took up the habit of spending his evenings sitting in front of the shop with the undertaker's apprentice. At first he used to come to him fully dressed in his suit and shoes; but after some time he gave this up, and saw no reason why he should not come out in slippers, and in the *gallabiyya* which he wore indoors. The apprentice's conversation was all about his work, its seasonal fluctuations, the glories it had known in the past, its pleasures and pains, its ritual and artistry, and the little tricks of his trade. One day he said to the young man:

"You're so interested in everything I say about it—you ask so many questions—you want to know so much; why don't you come with me next time we're sent for? I can say you're one of our boys. No one will be any wiser."

In his great boredom, he accepted the offer, and went indoors.

He had never seen a dead body before. They turned into a narrow, muddy alleyway, towards a house that stood shrouded in silence. When the people in the house noticed them, the building burst out in shrieks, wailings, the striking of cheeks in lamentation, and the pounding of feet upon the flat housetop; the house was behaving like a sick woman at an exorcism, when she hears the drumming of the exorcists starting up. At first, he was dumbfounded, and almost forgot himself so far as to clap his hands over his ears. Then he found himself threading his way through a crowd of small boys who were celebrating the obsequies with jollification: the discrepancy between the sounds and the boys' faces calmed him down. They clambered up a narrow staircase which the apprentice measured with his eyes, to estimate whether it was broad enough for the coffin. When they were inside the flat, the screaming and wailing, and the striking of cheeks, flared up once again, but in the middle of the uproar, his ears were able to distinguish the hiss of a primus stove, and he realized that they had not forgotten to put some water on the boil for the laying-out. Surrounded by tearful women in black headveils, he nevertheless had the impression that they were receiving him as they would receive a first-aid man. In fact, one old woman patted him on the back and said:

"Come on, sonny; you'll be wanting to get down to your work— and may God send you down His blessings."

He understood now how men of this profession could take a pride in their work and be contented with themselves. The apprentice drew him by the hand into a room where a corpse lay upon a mattress on the ground. He asked him to help carry the body to the bathroom, where the laying-out table, with a can of water upon the primus stove, had been placed, complete with jug and bowl, a luffa, and a piece of soap in readiness. But some of the members of the family were unwilling to allow a strange hand to touch the body until this was absolutely unavoidable, and so it was they themselves who carried it in on to the table: the apprentice then turned them out of the bathroom, allowing only one of them, an old man, to remain there reciting verses from the Koranic *Sura* of *Yassin*—for a laying-out is not canonical unless a witness is present.

With the deft hand of a pastry cook tossing a pancake, the undertaker's apprentice flung the white sheet off the corpse, so that it seemed to the young man like the wing of some legendary bird flapping above and around him, trying to touch him. Now that the cover had been removed, he stood for the first time face to face with a dead person.

Something that lies outside the division of things into three kingdoms, and forces on to you a new classification into two kingdoms that know no third: into corpses and non-corpses. A solid thing, and yet made of soft flesh, in the shape of a human being, and yet not human—and not animal either, or mineral. What affected him most was that when he looked at it, he could not tell whether he was confronted by a resignation which had reached the point of torment, or a torment carried so far that it passed into resignation. Was this dead body an arrested shriek, or was it the echo of a paean of praise? Was it a cry of jubilation which meant, "I am your servant, O my beloved!" Or was it a stifling of a moan which tried to say, "Enough, O Lord of mine!" Neither. It was simply nothing. And this thing which was no thing was in the form of a human being, but this was not a face that could be averted, this was not a mouth that would screw up in disdain, these were not arms that would push one away.

The young man's fear dissolved, and he fell to washing the corpse, gently, with a pitifulness that made the undertaker's apprentice lose his patience.

"Come on," he cried. "Hurry up—before they hide the counterpane from us."

It now became his habit to come down to the shop every day in *gallabiyya* and slippers; he insisted on accompanying the apprentice whenever he was sent for—in fact he would hurry to the address before the other did. A day that passed without a body seemed dull and colorless. He worked with the ardor of a passionate craftsman. His hands were eager to finger the merchandise all over. At first sight, all corpses may look much the same, but to the contemplative lover every one is different: Does it have open palms or clenched fists? Are the legs outstretched? Or are the knees bent, so that the legs are raised up stiffly towards the breast, like those of a newborn child, and the undertaker's apprentice has to press down upon them with all his weight in order to get the body into the coffin, and he sometimes wishes he had a hammer or a saw with him? A dwarf as heavy as lead. A giant as light as a feather. A corpse which is nothing more than rotting flesh upon decaying bones. Another which is a filled-out balloon. A face convulsed with fear. A face in repose, as though it were enjoying the calmest of rests.

The undertaker's apprentice realized that the young man could no longer leave him: he saw his smile becoming sweeter and gentler, and his eyes more languorous, while his body grew more softly pliable. When he sat with the young man now, he would sidle up right next to him, put his arm round his shoulders and then let it drop round his waist. Whenever he spoke to him, it would be in a whisper during which he held his mouth to the young man's ear. When he thought that his dish was cooked, he whispered one day:

"If you don't know what to do with yourself, just put yourself in my hands. Come on. Don't be standoffish. Don't be afraid. It's quite dark on the inside of the shop. And there's a big coffin there that'll take the two of us."

The young man brushed off these assaults, but he never complained or showed any anger: his thoughts were wandering in the dream kingdom of the grave.

The undertaker's apprentice resorted to a ruse which he had picked up from others of his kind. When the young man joined him on the day when he put it into operation, he made a point of keeping his distance, as though he had given up hope, or had come to his senses. He gave him no particular attention, but fell to making general reflections, cursing the times and regretting the old days. When he felt that the young man had been lulled into lowering his guard, he broke off his chatter and exclaimed that he had suddenly remembered a piece of news of prime importance.

"Have you heard? That woman who's our opposite number in the trade tells us that this blessed morning she's had the biggest day's takings that she's ever made in the trade and that she's ever likely to make in it to the end of her life. She was sent for to lay out a bride. Comes of a rich lot and was to have got married the next day. Her white dress was hanging up ready for her. The wedding attendant turned up and went into the bathroom with her to get her spruced up. She's hardly scrubbed her down, and she's just got up from beside the washstand to spray a bottle of scent over her, when she holds her hand to her heart and gives one sigh—and she's gone. They had music at the funeral, and they've strewn the ground over her grave with henna. And what's more, they insisted that she should have her wedding dress on, and her head wreathed with jasmine."

A bride in her first youth, bathed twice over and lying in her wedding gown with flowers strewn over her. And tonight a new moon.

"Fair or dark?" the young man asked with a catch in his throat.

"Dark. They say she may have come from Upper Egypt."

When he heard that, he jumped up and seized the undertaker's apprentice by the collar.

"Show me the way to her grave," he pleaded hoarsely.

And the man whispered back:

"On condition that you won't refuse, this time. On condition that you'll let me."

Two shadowy figures hurried off in the dark—a ravenous animal which would have swallowed gravel, and a broken, putrescent spirit from whom God had withdrawn His mercy.

One morning a message comes to the family from the hospital: their man of mark can no longer cut any figure in this world. His bed is empty, and waiting for a new occupant.

One of the most distinguished literary figures in Egypt, Yehia Hakki was born into a literary family in Cairo in 1905. He graduated from law school, worked as a lawyer, civil servant and diplomat in the Middle East and Western Europe before retiring to devote full time to writing. He was editor-in-chief of a monthly literary magazine for 10 years and is presently a member of the High Council of Literature and Art. "An Empty Bed" was translated by Mahmoud Manzalaoui and revised by Leonard Knight and Lewis Hall.

"Not the nervous type, are you?"

Summer and Miss Swanson

BY RICK FERREIRA

IT'S odd, I always think, just how people associate ghosts with dark mansions, cobwebs and creaking doors, and the graveyard at midnight. No one ever thinks, it seems, that a ghost can be a part of summer—as real as strong sun on your face, flowering gardens, or the quiet solidness of a leafy London Square. But then, *I* know that the traditional trappings aren't always necessary for a ghost to brush your life, briefly and strangely...for it was in summer that it happened.

Summer of '79, to be exact, and on that sweltering July day I found myself toiling up a hilly street that seemed to be heading straight for Hampstead Heath...but No. 42 turned out to be the last house but one—before a low wooden rail marked the start of endless grass and trees. The house was long and thin, a bit like the woman who opened the door to me and said rather sharply, "Yes?"

"I've come to see the attic flat," I said. "My name is Fairley. The

Agency should have phoned—"

She nodded then.

"Oh! I see. Well, come on in..." She seemed to have come to a favorable decision for the thin face split into a sudden—but friendly—smile. "Go on up and have a good look but it's five flights up. You're too young to be bothered by stairs, I'd say. I'll see you when you come down." She said something odd then—"Not the nervous type, are you? You know...*think* that you hear things at night? Attics aren't like other rooms, always a bit funny with creaks and things like that. I dare say you'll find it a bit ladylike, too...but I've decided *now* that a young man up there would be best. Well, you just knock on my sitting room door..."

So I started climbing up from the dim dusty hall that smelt of damp even on this blazing summer's day. And she was certainly right about the "ladylike" feel of the attic flat. The walls of the long low main room were papered in a leafy green pattern and the carpet was a pale blue. Most of the furniture was painted white and the bed looked too small, even for a midget. I climbed two shallow steps and came into the kitchen, tiny as a speedboat's galley. If you didn't eat much and kept your weight nice and steady, you could just turn around in it. *I* promptly knocked over the stool which should have been tucked under the breakfast-bar/kitchen table...

Then I saw the narrow door at the end of the kitchen and went over and drew back the bolt, and stepped out onto a little balcony. I found myself looking down on the tops of the trees that lined the street. Directly below, there was the flagstone path to the door of the house and when I looked to my right I saw that I had a marvelously sweeping view of the Heath. I was gazing at all that greenery, baking in the sunlight, when I felt that I wasn't alone on the small balcony. No cold wind on the back of my neck or anything as corny. I just knew, suddenly, that someone else *was* there. And the next moment that someone knocked the solitary flower-pot off the edge of the balcony wall!

I looked down, rather stupidly, at the broken bits of clay and scattered earth, far below on the path—with my arms still folded across my chest, as they had been since stepping on the balcony. And as I looked down I caught the small twin flashes of spectacles, uptilted. The face of the woman who had opened the door to me, was now peering up at the balcony, the lens of her glasses alight in the bright sun. Then suddenly she moved back into the shade of the porch and the twin flashes went out.

Odd. Very odd. No, I thought, the attic wasn't for me...

Finally, I went back into the main room and it looked more ladylike than ever, so I started down to the hall and found the thin face peering up, anxiously. *As well she might,* I thought. Then the anxious look vanished and the smile came back, but it wavered when I said, "Very kind of you to let me see the flat. But a girl would be far more right. And as for the bed—"

She pounced on *that.* "Well, I never did think that a gentleman your size could sleep on it. No—there'll be a new six-foot-two divan up there tonight. *And* I'll let you have it for two pounds weekly, electricity included. You won't get anything like that attic under six guineas—whatever that is in the new money. Not in Hampstead, you won't!" She must have seen that she had me for her smile grew more confident. "And what I don't see—you don't do! Well, Mr. Fairley?"

Well, what more was there to say? Except, "Yes. Yes. Thank you. If you're quite sure you can arrange about the bed...?" But I felt compelled to add, "But, look here, surely *two pounds* is far too—"

She cut me short by saying briskly:

"I've no intention of being the richest landlady in the graveyard!" And as briskly she set about giving me keys and filling in the rent-book, all of which she seemed to have at the ready. "Yes, a check will do, Mr. Fairley. Not usual with new tenants, but you look such a nice young man..."

The nice young man moved in the following evening, while the sun was slowly dying across the Heath. The new bed was big enough to accommodate all six-foot of me but I knew I'd find it hard to get on living terms with the wallpaper...still, after I dumped two crates of books on the carpet, opened a few suitcases, and generally chucked a few things around, I could see that the room would, eventually, get that real lived-in look.

Later, sitting on the stool in the tiny kitchen, I wrote out a list of the things I needed to buy to set up housekeeping proper. But even with the balcony door wide open, the kitchen was a small sweatbox, so I finally decided that priority No. 1 was to find that friendly neighborhood pub...

I found it at the foot of my winding street and it was called The Heathman—what else? I found the company congenial and the beer just right, so I stayed until closing time. And, miraculously, I made it safely up all those flights of stairs and tumbled headlong into bed. Some time in the night a storm broke and the rain lashed at the attic as if all hell mistook it for a stranded lighthouse. Thunder boomed and lightning flashed, but I was beery and warm...and in a moment I was asleep again. I came half awake when it had all died away to a soft drip-drip of rain, for someone, somewhere was crying. A gentle kind of sobbing that blended with the dying rain...but *that* was soothing, too, so again I drifted back to sleep.

I was shaving the next morning—with a not too steady hand—when I happened to look at the pad with my shopping list, still lying on the bar/table. My scrawled list had only taken up half the page so there was ample room for someone else to add a footnote.

And someone had done just *that*. In a neat clear hand—a nice "schoolteacher's hand" as my mother would have said—that someone had written: *Oh, why must it be like this? I'm so alone...*I peered closer and now I could see the rounded bumps on the paper that could have been dried tears! I finished my shaving rather hurriedly and went down to search out my landlady...

"Good morning. About my attic...could you please tell me something about the last tenant? I know it was a *girl*. Well, what made her move?"

She dropped one of the letters she had been sorting and I bent to pick it up but my head protested violently. As I came up, gingerly, I was suddenly swamped by a flood of words—"...and after *her*," said my landlady, "there was a Miss Peters, but she only stayed the one night, too!...Bed-sitter types, you know. Always moving—"

"But there was someone who lived up there for quite a while. Who is she?" I asked—*"And where is she now?"*

Suddenly, my landlady took a step closer and her free hand clutched my right arm, tightly. "Miss Swanson!" my landlady said. "That was her name and she was the last person you'd think would do such a thing. What she *did*, I mean. I mean, how was I to know? So quiet always and so respectable. In the Civil Service, you know—and she had the attic for over eight years. I even let her pick her own wallpaper and paint things but I didn't know just how she *felt* you see. How could anyone? The lonely part of it...I only knew afterwards, when I read the note. It's a month now and I can't get anyone to stay up there more than a single—" The phone in her sitting room startled us both by coming alive. "Oh, I must answer that," my landlady said. "Sorry, Mr. Fairley but I must go..."

And she went. But I wasn't altogether surprised that my landlady stayed out of sight when I came in that evening. She, very obviously, wasn't prepared to add to her outburst of the morning...to add that vital little bit of information that would complete the sad story. Just how had Miss Swanson—well—done it? I knew the *why* of it, and that whatever way she had ended her life, she was still brooding on her continuing loneliness. So I came to a decision...

Just before bedtime, I wrote on my pad on the bar/table in my tiny kitchen: *I'd like to help you, if I can. There's no need to cry. How can you be lonely when I'm always around?* Somehow, I didn't find any of this strange, or even mildly frightening. Miss Swanson didn't seem that kind of ghost.

Then I fell asleep on the top of the bed for it was far too warm to get between sheets...even though I had the balcony door wide open. But the door brought me awake some time after midnight for it was banging away like mad, in a sudden cool wind that had sprung up. I got up, practically sleepwalking, and stumbled up to the kitchen, my hand searching for the light-switch. But I stopped...for I could see that someone was sitting upright on the stool, clear and distinct, in the soft night-glow from the balcony.

Then the door banged shut for a moment, darkening the small kitchen and when the wind again banged it open, Miss Swanson had stood up and started moving slowly out to the balcony. And she was exactly as I had pictured her: small, neat, dark-haired, the faint light glowing on her glasses. She went quietly past me, out to the balcony, paused a moment, then, like a diver trying out the highboard for the first time, Miss Swanson threw herself very violently out into the windy darkness. She may have screamed, that first time, but now she made no sound. It was all like a film-clip from an old silent movie and, as when I'd first heard her story, I felt only a deep regret that sheer loneliness could have driven anyone to do *that*...

I knew that I would see nothing on the path below if I went out on the balcony, so I bolted the door against the wind then, finally, switched on the light. Right away I could see that there had been a written addition to the pad on the bar/table. I bent close, once again admiring the neat hand of the late Miss Swanson. She had written: *Thank you for your kind offer. It was all I needed. Good-bye.* There were no tear-stains, wet or dry. I knew then that I had seen and heard the last of her...

Well, yes—and no.

I stayed on for five years in that attic flat and my landlady and I never spoke again of Miss Swanson. My rent stayed at two pounds (electricity included), and I did exactly as I liked. For the other tenants there were rules, but none for the ghost-haunted Mr. Fairley!

But I finally moved last week...to a bachelor flat in a new service block. Summer seems to be moving time for me. And for someone else.

On my first night in the new flat, that someone wrote an addition to my shopping list, in her neat, unmistakable hand. Next morning I read what the late Miss Swanson had written:

I think I shall like it here. I'm never lonely now. So lovely to know that I shall never be again!

I did say something nice and evocative, at the very beginning. Remember?—"...A ghost can brush your life, briefly and strangely..." Well, strangely, anyway.

I must now learn to live with the knowledge that the late Miss Swanson will be with me, a bit more than briefly. For all the summers left to me, in fact. And, rather odd this, I find the idea, somehow, *comforting.*

Born in Tobago in 1926, Rick Ferreira emigrated to London in 1954, "exchanging eternal sunshine for first glimpse of snow." He has been writing since early childhood: poems, articles, book reviews, stories, novels. His stories appear in English magazines and his own collections. His work also appears on TV and radio.

"I get no satisfaction in winning by cheating."

A Kind of Madness

BY E.G. CHIPULINA

THE bungalow that the company had allotted to Ramon Urtali and his wife Laura overlooked the village of Los Naranjos, whose name derived from the orange grove atop the headland that sheltered it from the sea. Torrevieja oil refinery, where Ramon worked, rose out of the sandy shoreline on the opposite side of the bay. Sitting in his veranda, he could just glimpse the nearest of the other bungalows squatting amid the scraggy olive trees and rosemary bushes growing wild down the slope. It had been occupied the previous day by the newly-arrived couple, the Fentons, who were his guests that evening. Laura was in the kitchen preparing canapes—with a frown on her face; all day long she'd been preoccupied with what Mrs. Fenton would be wearing—was she young, pretty?

"They're just ordinary folk," Ramon had reassured her. But the truth was his new colleague's wife had seemed far from ordinary when he'd gone to pick them up at the airport. He could smell trouble ahead. Middle-age had made Laura prone to tedious fits of jealousy. She didn't consider him past the age of mischief merely because he had put on weight and shed most of his hair. Lost in these reflections he almost missed the Fentons, who were slowly coming up the pathway from their bungalow.

He jumped up, scurrying out of sight. "Laura! Laura, they're coming!" She'd never forgive him if they surprised her with her apron on.

"Wait!" said Laura when she heard their knock. "Don't make it so obvious you've been on the lookout." Ramon sighed and waited what he reckoned should be a decent interval, then opened the door—what idiotic things one had to do for the sake of domestic peace!

"My dear Gerald!" He turned from his new colleague to bow to the blonde young woman at his side, who seemed if possible more desirable in the half-light than she had in the midday glare at the airport. "Do come in. I was afraid you'd lose your way in the wilderness."

Her big blue eyes opened with a sort of fake baby look. "I hope you meant to come and look for us." Before Ramon could even laugh, she spotted Laura coming up behind him and swept past him with outstretched hands. "Mrs. Urtali!" she exclaimed with great charm, dispensing with the formalities. "How very nice to meet you!"

The spectacle of two women sizing each other up for the first time always amused Ramon. During the exchange of compliments, he cast a discreet glance at his colleague who was patiently waiting to be introduced. British and American technical men—as he'd had ample opportunity to observe during twenty years in the industry—tended to be fairly uncomplicated, practical beings. But there was a certain sensitivity about this one's features, and that evasive inward gaze, which didn't quite fit somehow. As soon as the introductions were over he took him aside.

"Leave the women to their babbling for a bit," he winked. "What will you drink?"

"Er...whatever it is you're having."

"Sherry, perhaps?" He turned to the women. "Mrs. Fenton, what would you care to drink?"

"Sherry for me, please. But do call me Vanessa."

"Very well, then, sherry for Vanessa too." In his eagerness to get the party going, he poured the same for Laura without asking. She'd probably have something to say about that later.

They drifted out to the coolness of the veranda. To Ramon's ear, Vanessa's ecstatic praise of Laura's canapes had a ring of calculated flattery, but Laura seemed to be lapping it up. They had dinner out in the veranda too, and Ramon felt the mood of the company augured well for their future relationship. In the distance, where the curve of the bay ended abruptly, Torrevieja rose in a confused skyline of twisted pipes and lofty stacks. A flare burning off waste gas created an artificial sunset scene mirrored in the still waters. The massed lights that brought a weird sort of gaiety to the desolate landscape were already twinkling palely like emerging stars.

"There are moments," mused Ramon, "when the refinery does not seem quite the eyesore it is accused of being."

Vanessa agreed a little breathlessly, as if anxious to show she had aesthetic sense. "But then there's beauty everywhere if you care to see it, don't you think?"

It tickled Ramon to see Laura suddenly taking a perplexed interest in a scene she'd witnessed so many times with a blind eye.

"I wonder," said Fenton, as if talking to himself, "what the people down there in Los Naranjos think."

There was a momentary silence. The remark seemed to warrant some kind of answer but no one took him up. The conversation went off at a tangent. Laura began to clear the dinner table and Vanessa insisted in helping with the washing up. The two men were left silently sipping brandy.

"Normally," said Ramon dryly, "I do the washing up but she'd rather die than admit it publicly."

Fenton smiled, gazing absently towards the sea. Night was fast falling on the scene with the glow from the refinery silhouetting a large crude carrier on the centipede jetty reaching out beyond the shallows.

Ramon refilled their glasses. "The *Serafina* should have finished unloading by now," he observed. "A fine ship, that—from the economic viewpoint, anyway. She is—how do you say it?—ugly as sin."

Fenton nodded. "I served on a tanker very like her once."

Really? You mean with the company fleet?"

"Yes. As an engineer officer."

"Life at sea didn't agree with you, then?"

"Oh, yes, I loved it."

While Ramon was considering if it would seem inquisitive to ask the next obvious question, Fenton anticipated and said, "It's not...er...quite the same when you're married, you understand?"

"Of course." Ramon understood only too well. It was definitely not quite the same, especially if one happened to be married to a woman like Vanessa. He tactfully dropped the subject; his sharp ears had caught a trace of embarrassment in Fenton's voice.

The confused chirping of insects in the stillness of the countryside seemed to mimic the ceaseless chatter reaching them from the kitchen. Laura, so often tongue-tied among foreigners, seemed to be waxing eloquent tonight. Did women ever listen to each other? wondered Ramon. He felt an upsurge of sympathy for the man beside him, who seemed content to keep silent when there was nothing to say.

The Fentons left about midnight. There hadn't been a single contretemps all evening. It was obvious to Ramon that Vanessa had made a great impression on Laura. And, undoubtedly, the woman had other charms besides a pretty face and a voluptuous body. Still, it was charm of the suave, self-assured sort that he instinctively distrusted.

Several weeks later Ramon came home with the news that the Chief Maintenance Engineer, an Australian called MacKenzie, had been taken seriously ill with ulcers, and Laura became all agog speculating about who might take his place.

"They'll probably bring someone in," explained Ramon. "The rest of us are on short-term contract."

"Gerald, too?" she said.

"I'm not sure about him."

"I think Vanessa has hopes Gerald will get a promotion soon."

"She said that?"

"Well...implied it, anyway."

Ramon thoughtfully poured himself a glass of wine. "I don't think Gerald is all that experienced."

"Well, she strikes me as an ambitious person—not in the wrong sense, mind you, for his sake, you know."

For a moment he was afraid of a sudden resurgence of Laura's own dormant ambitions—he'd had his share of that over the years—but her thoughts seemed to flit elsewhere.

"Vanessa's very beautiful," she said. "Don't you agree?"

Careful now, he thought, she could be very sly sometimes. He grunted non-committally as he took a sip of wine.

Laura gave him a supercilious glance. "Don't tell me you haven't noticed!"

A resounding crash of breaking crockery came from the kitchen. Laura touched her brow with a horrified expression. As she hurried off to investigate, Ramon blessed the young maid from the village for her timely incompetence.

The man who was to take MacKenzie's place arrived the following week and was introduced by the manager to the maintenance staff in the offices adjoining the main workshop. Maxwell Coleman was British, though visibly of mixed parentage. Tall and elegant, handsome in a sallow way with a trim black moustache and not a hair out of place, he so reminded Ramon of a screen gallant of several decades ago whom he'd particularly despised that he became prejudiced against him from the start. Not that it much bothered Ramon; he had long since learned to work with people he disliked. But he was struck by the contrast with his former boss. Old MacKenzie had had his faults like everybody else, but he'd been an ungainly, unassuming man, very matter-of-fact—a breed Ramon knew and understood. Coleman, with his too-ready toothy smile and air of being immensely interested in what other people had to say, seemed somehow misplaced—more cut out for a job in public relations.

Apropos of which, one of the first things he did was to throw a party—an exercise in familiarization, as he confidentially put it to Ramon. The only bachelor in the bungalow colony, Coleman turned

SHORT STORY INTERNATIONAL

out to be—not altogether surprisingly—a ladies man to boot. He charmed the women present with his choice little gallantries and caused a mild stir when he modestly admitted to having prepared the food for the party himself. Not that he in any way neglected his male guests. Even when the party had reached the stage when most people have had too much to drink, Coleman remained sober and correct, still bubbling with serious conversation and evidently not in the least put out by his listeners' glazed eyes and dull nodding. Ramon, who was a keen observer of the idiosyncracies of his fellow beings, missed no detail. He could gauge Coleman's sex appeal by the look on his own wife's face when she spoke to him—which didn't matter very much because he felt too old for jealousy. But he couldn't help wondering what was going through Fenton's mind. It was plain to see that Vanessa, way out the most attractive woman present, was getting the lion's share of their host's attention, and that Vanessa was responding like a flower to sunlight. Moreover, he had a feeling that the situation was not new to Fenton.

At work the following morning, when Fenton met his tentative remarks about their new boss with evasion, Ramon sensed his friend's antipathy went deeper than his own—and for a more tangible reason. It wasn't long, however, before Coleman proved Ramon mistaken in one respect: he seemed to know his job. Tacitly implying that his predecessor's methods had been slipshod, he tightened up discipline, streamlined maintenance schedules, and kept on the move all day in the land-rover—with an expression of boundless patience on his face, his smile, however toothy, always forthcoming.

Nor did it take Coleman long to make an impact on the sluggish society of Los Naranjos estate. An active man with a keen competitive sense, he seemed to inspire others with his enthusiasm and soon gathered about him a band of converts to his way of doing things. Ramon, who loved spending a lazy afternoon in the bay on a hired fishing boat, caring little whether he caught anything or not, found himself out of step with the new trend. Fishing, including the underwater variety, became a fiercely competitive sport requiring the catch to be weighed and recorded. Bridge, hitherto a mere excuse for getting together, was organized on tournament lines. In fact, Coleman had a finger in every pie.

Ramon found himself being taken to task by Laura for declining to participate in all this hectic activity. She accused him of being childish, unsporting—even jealous of Coleman. Which he thought quite laughable. But again, when he learned that Fenton too had opted out, he wondered if his friend took the same light-hearted view of things. It seemed Vanessa had become one of Coleman's most ardent disciples, and whether by accident or design, she was partnering him at bridge.

Apart from driving occasionally into Larios, the nearest town, there was a quicker, simpler means of a little diversion from the somewhat introverted social life of Los Naranjos. Some evenings Ramon would walk down the winding path to the village and watch the fishermen hauling in their nets on the beach. The primitive spectacle satisfied him, and if he fancied any fish, it could be had for next to nothing. He often ran into Fenton in the village, usually sitting alone at a rickety table outside the cafe on the tiny square, and they would share a bottle or two of cheap red wine. Fenton was not very eloquent, and betrayed a shy nature by the way he tended to express himself obliquely. But Ramon somehow understood him. One evening, as they watched the fisher folk cooking a meal on the beach with the tantalizing smell of barbecued sardines wafting across on the breeze, Fenton remarked:

"I can never make up my mind whether to pity or envy these people."

Ramon shrugged and said, deliberately to draw him out, "What is there to envy about poverty?"

"Yes, that's true, yet..."

"What?"

"Life seems so uncomplicated for them. Do you think *they're* bothered by ambition?"

"I doubt it."

"And they're tough, too."

"Well, they work hard enough."

"No, I mean in another sense. They don't hurt easily—like we do."

Fenton never became personal. He always remained concealed behind these generalizations. But from the glimpses Ramon managed to get of him he built up an impression of a very unhappy man. Perhaps Vanessa's persistent association with Coleman was at the root of the trouble—tongues were beginning to wag at Los Naranjos. Fenton was obviously very much in love with his wife, and perhaps she did not return his love. Possibly everything had been fine between them once, yet essentially they struck him as so out of tune with each other. Why, he reflected sadly, does a man insist on becoming passionately obsessed with a woman who is clearly temperamentally unsuited to him?

One morning at work Ramon found a summons scribbled on his pad and, knocking perfunctorily, entered the office adjoining his. From behind an outsize desk Coleman looked up through the heavy-rimmed spectacles he reserved exclusively for the office.

"Ah, Ramon, do sit down...dump those files anywhere—no, not on the floor—here, that's it!"

Ramon sat gratefully in the draught of the air conditioner. Sunlight reflecting on the aluminum-painted machinery across the way filtered in through the plastic blinds.

Have you seen Gerald today?" asked Coleman.

"No, I must have missed him on his way out. Why?"

"Then obviously you don't know."

"Know what?"

Coleman rose and began to pace to and fro. "Something very unpleasant happened this morning, I'm afraid."

"You mean an accident?"

Coleman shook his head emphatically. "About eight, I drove here with the shift foreman to pick up the two stand-by men, who were needed for the insulation job in the control room. We found them fighting like animals in the middle of the road—out there!" He gestured towards the window.

"Who were they?"

"Perez and Nabarro."

"Hmmm! I'm not surprised about Nabarro. He's a surly, quarrelsome bastard."

"Well it took all my authority and the foreman's muscle to get him off the other man." Coleman wagged a warning finger. "Now, I won't tolerate that sort of thing in my outfit."

Ramon dutifully agreed. Coleman gave an emphatic little cough. "Anyway, the point is that Gerald was just sitting there in his office doing absolutely nothing to restore order."

"Maybe he wasn't aware what was happening," suggested Ramon.

"Come, come, my dear fellow! With those two rolling on the ground just outside his window—and Nabarro roaring like a madman?"

"Most unusual," conceded Ramon. "Did you ask him about it?"

"Of course. But he simply stared at me in a most peculiar way—I just couldn't get a straight answer from him. I can understand his not feeling equal to the task of separating those two, but surely he could have summoned help. I mean...the whole thing's downright irresponsible!"

Ramon scratched his bald pate perplexedly. He didn't relish having to agree with Coleman.

"Besides," continued the other, "he's sure to have heard the quarrel building up before they actually came to blows. Nabarro is loud-mouthed enough. A quick-witted man would have nipped the thing in the bud." He paused as if to allow his words to sink in. "Now, I have a great regard for Gerald, but I assure you I've had to stretch my tolerance close to breaking point not to write a stiffly-worded report on the matter." He gazed at Ramon with a faintly womanish air of indignation, as if expecting some comment. When none came, he added: "Very well, that's all Ramon. I just thought you should know. And please! Keep this to yourself."

Ramon left the office without a doubt in his mind that Coleman hoped he would privately tell Fenton of his magnanimity. But he hadn't the slightest intention of causing his friend any embarrassment. As far as he was concerned the matter was closed.

To his surprise, however, Fenton himself raised the subject the next time they happened to meet at the village cafe.

"I suppose," he said with an air of resignation, "Coleman told you about the fight incident."

Ramon decided it would serve no purpose to feign ignorance. "Yes, he did mention it."

"I thought he would."

"He told me his version, anyway."

"It's the only version there is," said Fenton dryly. "I shan't dispute his report."

"I gather he doesn't intend to make one."

"He told you that?"

Ramon nodded. "In confidence, of course."

The irony in his voice did not escape Fenton. "Yes," he said bitterly, "I have to feel grateful to him for that."

As they continued drinking in silence Ramon wished he could think of something to say that would comfort him, but the rhythm of the surf and the glare from the offshore haze seemed to dull his wits. Then Fenton's quiet voice snapped him out of his lethargy.

"Why don't you ask what you're thinking? You don't have to be so tactful, you know."

Ramon felt suddenly uncomfortable. "I don't need any explanations, my friend."

"Maybe not, but I'd still feel better for having told you."

"Told me—what?"

"Oh, come on, Ramon, you know perfectly well what I mean."

He was right, of course, but Ramon couldn't think of anything to deviate from the subject.

Fenton continued, "You see I've always had this revulsion to violence."

"I suppose most of us have."

Fenton considered for a moment. "Morally, perhaps. But in my case it's a purely physical thing. I mean, I'm not a Quaker or anything like that." He paused, then suddenly became excited. "Look, I tell you I feel physically sick at the sight of two human beings battering each other with murder in their eyes...yes, capable of murdering each other over a trivial disagreement..."

"Easy, my friend!" said Ramon soothingly. "There are usually psychological reasons for these things—nothing to be ashamed of."

"Of course I'm ashamed," said Fenton scornfully. "You talk about psychology—how can I redeem myself with values I don't understand? Who understands psychology, anyway? The only values I know are the ones I was brought up with. I get no satisfaction in winning by cheating."

Ramon was a little taken aback by the passion in his voice. "I think you're making too much of all this," he said lamely.

Fenton ignored him, mumbling to himself, "I'm just an unmitigated coward making excuses."

Ramon couldn't come up with anything to counter Fenton's self-reproach. He wanted desperately to help his friend, and felt the opportunity to do so slipping from his grasp, with a premonition that it would never come again.

With his shirttail trailing behind him and Laura's warning cries ringing in his ears, Ramon scampered down the steep path from his bungalow to the clearing where, neatly parked under a reed canopy, stood the cars of the residents of Los Naranjos. Across the bay a dense black column of smoke reared up from the refinery, an ugly stain on the delicate hues of the dawn sky. It was difficult to determine the exact location of the explosion that had shaken him from sleep, but he guessed it was somewhere in the small outer tank park.

Other men, half-dressed like himself, appeared on the crest of the hill as he drove off in a cloud of dust along the track that linked up with the highway. Five minutes later, where uneven country briefly blocked his view of Torrevieja, a heavy thud—as if a boulder had fallen on the roof of his car—announced a second explosion. When he emerged into the flatland, the twin column of smoke that met his anxious gaze was now close enough to confirm his first estimate of the site of the accident. And he knew exactly how near it was to the compressor house where some of his maintenance colleagues had been carrying out emergency repairs. When Fenton had relieved him late last night, there had been two mechanics on the job, and Coleman was sure to have been in the offing.

Once he got to the refinery road, with men running here and there, he almost collided with an oncoming ambulance. At the turning that led to the tank park he was waved down by a man with a red flag. Ramon parked on one side and went ahead on foot. The heat and the stink of burning gasoline grew overpowering. When the two adjacent blazing tanks came in full view round the corner of the towering cat-cracker, he realized the fire fighters were already in control. Luck was on their side, for the relatively isolated position of the tanks and the absence of wind made the danger of further explosions minimal. Then he noticed with a shock that the compressor house had been razed by the blast.

He tried to find out from the men helping the fire fighters what had happened, but no one seemed sure except that there had been several casualties. At last he found one of his own men who told him that Fenton and one of the mechanics working on the compressor had been killed, while a mechanic called Ferrat had been injured. Not wanting to believe him, Ramon searched everywhere for Coleman, who was the man likely to know all the facts, but the boss was nowhere to be found. After one more look at the dwindling fire, and deciding there was little he could usefully do at this stage, he hurried to the first-aid post in case they still had Ferrat. He was told the wounded man had been taken to the Larios Municipal Hospital. They knew nothing about either Fenton or Coleman. All the other casualties they had treated had been for minor injuries.

Ramon hung about uncertainly for a while; then on an impulse he returned to his car and set off towards Larios. He still had a forlorn hope that he'd been misinformed about Fenton, and Ferrat was probably the only man who could give him a first-hand account of the incident.

When he finally reached the hospital, he had difficulty in persuading a little white nun to let him see Ferrat.

"Ten minutes only," she said severely, "and on no account must you upset him."

"I promise not to, Sister."

A strong smell of disinfectant hit him as he followed the nun down a long ward where, in a corner bed behind a screen, lay Ferrat. He looked livid and dazed, but the only sign of injury was a small sticking-plaster on his cheek. His dull eyes lit up with recognition as Ramon leaned over him, with a cheerful: "Well, well, how are you man?"

"Alive," said Ferrat, grinning weakly, "alive!" He took Ramon's hand. "It was good of you to come."

He was a tough, dependable little man, and Ramon felt slightly hypocritical because he had really come to find out what had happened to Fenton. "Are you in pain?" he asked.

"Nothing much." He craned his neck to squint down the length of the bed. "What worries me is that there is no feeling at all in my right leg. Do you think...I will lose it?"

"Come now, you mustn't talk like that."

"Why not? What does it matter? I am lucky to be here at all—at someone else's expense..."

Ramon hushed him. "Please don't excite yourself or the nun will throw me out. Do you recall what happened, or would you rather not talk?"

"Of course I will talk— I *must* talk..."

"Easy, easy!" Ramon gently patted his arm. "Tell me, how did the explosion happen?"

"I think the tank overflowed. We were working in the compressor house when my mate Hernandez smelt gasoline fumes. He shouted to Mr. Coleman who was walking away towards the land-rover with Mr. Fenton. But it was the last thing he ever said. Part of the roof suddenly collapsed and buried him. I was luckier, but my legs were trapped by falling masonry."

"Could you see what happened to Mr. Fenton?"

"Mr. Fenton?" Ferrat stared into space, then pointed. "He was there, lying on the ground, and the chief."

"You mean...knocked out?"

"No. They were both getting up, slowly, staring at me as if I were a ghost."

"Were either of them wounded, do you think?"

"No, not even wounded. You see, it was the small tank, the one farthest from the compressor house, that had exploded. If it had been the big one we would all of us have been blown sky high."

Ferrat screwed his eyes with the effort of recalling every detail of his nightmarish experience. Ramon didn't press him, and kept glancing round the screen for any sign of the nun.

"I was too stunned to be afraid," continued Ferrat unprompted. "But I could feel the heat building up and I knew the big tank was going to blow up any minute. Mr. Coleman was running towards the truck, but Mr. Fenton was just standing there, motionless. I thought at first perhaps his legs were hurt. But no, he took a firm step back and started yelling and waving to the chief to come back. The other just ignored him and jumped into the truck—of course he wanted to get the hell out of there. But Mr. Fenton kept yelling at him like a man possessed. I don't understand their language well enough but what he was saying were insults in any tongue." Ferrat paused to shrug his shoulders. "He could have saved his breath. The chief was soon speeding away down the road."

Ramon considered for a moment. But the other tank *had* exploded. How was it possible that this man was here telling him all this? Ferrat answered his question.

"The next thing I remember is that Mr. Fenton was heaving away the chunks of cement that trapped my legs. He seemed to have superhuman strength. He was swearing all the time, and I don't think he was aware of me as a person. When my legs were free, he hooked me under the armpits and dragged me away. The nearest likely shelter was the thermal cracking plant, but that's a hell of a long way to drag a dead weight. Luckily there was this trench by the roadside where they were looking for a fault in the electric cables. He dumped me in there."

The white nun appeared suddenly in the gap between the screen and the wall. "Your time is up, Señor." She took one look at her patient, then said accusingly, "There, you see? You have made him excited."

"Sister," said Ferrat, like a little boy pleading, "one more minute, please!"

A smile briefly softened her austere face. "Very well, then, one minute. I shall be back."

"She's not bad really," smiled Ferrat. He remained gazing absently at Ramon for several seconds. "Ah, yes! He dumped me there and was gone. After a while—I don't know why; perhaps this curiosity that sometimes kills us—I heaved myself up with great difficulty and managaed to peer over the top of the trench." Ferrat shook his head slowly. "I still can't believe it. No man in his right senses would have done that. It would have needed a crane or a bulldozer to move that mountain of rubble that had buried Hernandez. Mr. Fenton was trying it with his bare hands."

They remained silent for a moment, Ramon gazing reflectively at the face of the injured man. No sign of delirium there, he decided, nor any kind of unbalance. But his story was difficult to credit.

"You know," mused Ferrat, "I owe Mr. Fenton my life, but I don't think he was really a brave man. It was more as if...well, as if a kind of madness had suddenly taken hold of him.

The multi-talented Gibraltarian E.G. Chipulina has a love for language and literature closely matched by his love for painting and sketching. He has been writing about 20 years, mostly short stories and historical articles which are published in prestigious magazines. He always credits his cheerful wife with actively encouraging him to turn from his first profession, accounting, to writing. Mr. Chipulina was first introduced in SSI No. 13 with "The Man on the Gray Horse" and is scheduled to appear in future SSI issues.

"With what...with what do you have ties?"

The Name

BY AHARON MEGGED

GRANDFATHER Zisskind lived in a little house in a southern suburb of the town. About once a month, on a Saturday afternoon, his granddaughter Raya and her young husband Yehuda would go and pay him a visit.

Raya would give three cautious knocks on the door (an agreed signal between herself and her grandfather ever since her childhood, when he had lived in their house together with the whole family) and they would wait for the door to be opened. "Now he's getting up," Raya would whisper to Yehuda, her face glowing, when the sound of her grandfather's slippers was heard from within, shuffling across the room. Another moment, and the key would be turned and the door opened.

"Come in," he would say somewhat absently, still buttoning up his trousers, with the rheum of sleep in his eyes. Although it was very hot he wore a yellow winter vest with long sleeves, from which his wrists stuck out—white, thin, delicate as a girl's, as was his bare neck with its taut skin.

After Raya and Yehuda had sat down at the table, which was covered with a white cloth showing signs of the meal he had eaten alone—crumbs from the Sabbath loaf, a plate with meat leavings, a glass containing some grape pips, a number of jars and so on—he would smooth the crumpled pillows, spread a cover over the narrow bed and tidy up. It was a small room, and its obvious disorder aroused pity for the old man's helplessness in running his home. In the corner was a shelf with two sooty kerosene burners, a kettle and two or three saucepans, and next to it a basin containing plates, knives and forks. In another corner was a stand holding books with thick leather bindings, leaning and lying on each other. Some of his clothes hung over the backs of the chairs. An ancient walnut cupboard with an empty buffet stood exactly opposite the door. On the wall hung a clock which had long since stopped.

"We ought to make Grandfather a present of a clock," Raya would say to Yehuda as she surveyed the room and her glance lighted on the clock; but every time the matter slipped her memory. She loved her grandfather, with his pointed white silky beard, his tranquil face from which a kind of holy radiance emanated, his quiet, soft voice which seemed to have been made only for uttering words of sublime wisdom. She also respected him for his pride, which had led him to move out of her mother's house and live by himself, accepting the hardship and trouble and the affliction of loneliness in his old age. There had been a bitter quarrel between him and his daughter. After Raya's father had died, the house had lost its grandeur and shed the trappings of wealth. Some of the antique furniture which they had retained—along with some crystalware and jewels, the dim luster of memories from the days of plenty in their native city—had been sold, and Rachel, Raya's mother, had been compelled to support the home by working as a dentist's nurse. Grandfather Zisskind, who had been supported by the family ever since he came to the country, wished to hand over to his daughter his small capital, which was deposited in a bank. She was not willing to accept it. She was stubborn and proud like him. Then, after a prolonged quarrel and several weeks of not speaking to each other, he took some of the things in his room and the broken clock and went to live alone. That had been about four years ago. Now Rachel would come to him once or twice a week, bringing with her a bag full of provisions, to clean the room and cook some meals for him. He was no longer interested in expenses and did not even ask about them, as though they were of no more concern to him.

"And now...what can I offer you?" Grandfather Zisskind would ask when he considered the room ready to receive guests. "There's no need to offer us anything, Grandfather; we didn't come for that," Raya would answer crossly.

But protests were of no avail. Her grandfather would take out a jar of fermenting preserves and put it on the table, then grapes and plums, biscuits and two glasses of strong tea, forcing them to eat. Raya would taste a little of this and that just to please the old man, while Yehuda, for whom all these visits were unavoidable torment, the very sight of the dishes arousing his disgust, would secretly indicate to her by pulling a sour face that he just couldn't touch the preserves. She would smile at him placatingly, stroking his knee. But Grandfather insisted, so he would have to taste at least a teaspoonful of the sweet and nauseating stuff.

Afterwards Grandfather would ask about all kinds of things. Raya did her best to make the conversation pleasant, in order to relieve Yehuda's boredom. Finally would come what Yehuda dreaded most of all and on account of which he had resolved more than once to refrain from these visits. Grandfather Zisskind would rise, take his chair and place it next to the wall, get up on it carefully, holding on to the back so as not to fall, open the clock and take out a cloth bag with a black cord tied round it. Then he would shut the clock, get off the chair, put it back in its place, sit down on it, undo the cord, take out of the cloth wrapping a bundle of sheets of paper, lay them in front of Yehuda and say:

"I would like you to read this."

"Grandfather," Raya would rush to Yehuda's rescue, "but he's already read it at least ten times..."

But Grandfather Zisskind would pretend not to hear and would not reply, so Yehuda was compelled each time to read there and then that same essay, spread over eight, long sheets in a large, somewhat shaky handwriting, which he almost knew by heart. It was a lament for Grandfather's native town in the Ukraine which had been destroyed by the Germans, and all its Jews slaughtered. When he had finished, Grandfather would take the sheets out of his hand, fold them, sigh and say:

"And nothing of all this is left. Dust and ashes. Not even a tombstone to bear witness. Imagine, of a community of twenty thousand Jews not even one survived to tell how it happened...Not a trace."

Then out of the same cloth bag, which contained various letters and envelopes, he would draw a photograph of his grandson Mendele, who had been twelve years old when he was killed; the only son of his son Ossip, chief engineer in a large chemical factory. He would show it to Yehuda and say:

"He was a genius. Just imagine, when he was only eleven he had already finished his studies at the Conservatory, won a scholarship from the Government and was considered an outstanding violinist. A genius! Look at that forehead..." And after he had put the photograph back he would sigh and repeat "Not a trace."

A strained silence of commiseration would descend on Raya and Yehuda, who had already heard these same things many times over and no longer felt anything when they were repeated. And as he wound the cord round the bag the old man would muse: "And Ossip was also a prodigy. As a boy he knew Hebrew well, and could recite Bialik's poems by heart. He studied by himself. He read endlessly, Gnessin, Frug, Bershadsky...You didn't know Bershadsky; he was a good writer...He had a warm heart, Ossip had. He didn't mix in politics, he wasn't even a Zionist, but even when they promoted him there he didn't forget that he was a Jew...He called his son Mendele, of all names, after his dead brother, even though it was surely not easy to have a name like that among the Russians...Yes, he had a warm Jewish heart..."

He would turn to Yehuda as he spoke, since in Raya he always saw the child who used to sit on his knee listening to his stories, and for him she had never grown up, while he regarded Yehuda as an educated man who could understand someone else, especially inasmuch as Yehuda held a government job.

Raya remembered how the change had come about in her grandfather. When the war was over he was still sustained by uncertainty and hoped for some news of his son, for it was known that very many had succeeded in escaping eastwards. Wearily he would visit all those who had once lived in his town, but none of them had received any sign of life from relatives. Nevertheless he continued to hope, for Ossip's important position might have helped to save him. Then Raya came home one evening and saw him sitting on the floor with a rent in his jacket. In the house they spoke in whispers, and her mother's eyes were red with weeping. She, too, had wept at Grandfather's sorrow, at the sight of his stricken face, at the oppressive quiet in the rooms. For many weeks afterwards it was as if he had imposed silence on himself. He would sit at his table from morning to night, reading and re-reading old letters, studying family photographs by the hour as he brought them close to his shortsighted eyes, or leaning backwards on his chair, motionless, his hand touching the edge of the table and his eyes staring through the window in front of him, into the distance, as if he had turned to stone. He was no longer the same talkative, wise and humorous grandfather who interested himself in the house, asked what his granddaughter was doing, instructed her, tested her knowledge, proving boastfully like a child that he knew more than her teachers. Now he seemed to cut himself off from the world and entrench himself in his thoughts and his memories, which none of the household could penetrate. Later, a strange perversity had taken hold of him which it was hard to tolerate. He would insist that his meals be served at his table, apart, that no one should enter his room without knocking at the door, or close the shutters of his window against the sun. When any one disobeyed these prohibitions he would flare up and quarrel violently with his daughter. At times it seemed that he hated her.

When Raya's father died, Grandfather Zisskind did not show any signs of grief, and did not even console his daughter. But when the days of mourning were past it was as if he had been restored to new life, and he emerged from his silence. Yet he did not speak of his son-in-law, nor of his son Ossip, but only of his grandson Mendele. Often during the day he would mention the boy by name as if he were alive, and speak of him familiarly, although he had seen him only on photographs—as though deliberating aloud and turning the matter over, he would talk of how Mendele ought to be brought up. It was hardest of all when he started criticizing his son and his son's wife for not having foreseen the impending disaster, for not having rushed the boy away to a safe place, not having hidden him with non-Jews, not having tried to get him to the Land of Israel in good time. There was no logic in what he said; this would so infuriate Rachel that she would burst out with, "Oh, do stop! Stop it! I'll go out of my mind with your foolish nonsense!" She would rise from her seat in anger, withdraw to her room, and afterwards, when she had calmed down, would say to Raya, "Sclerosis, apparently. Loss of memory. He no longer knows what he's talking about."

One day—Raya would never forget this—she and her mother saw that Grandfather was wearing his best suit, the black one, and under it a gleaming white shirt; his shoes were polished, and he had a hat on. He had not worn these clothes for many months, and the family was dismayed to see him. They thought that he had lost his mind. "What holiday is it today?" her mother asked. "Really, don't you know?" asked her grandfather. "Today is Mendele's birthday!" Her mother burst out crying. She too began to cry and ran out of the house.

After that, Grandfather Zisskind went to live alone. His mind, apparently, had become settled, except that he would frequently forget things which had occurred a day or two before, though he clearly remembered, down to the smallest detail, things which had happened in his town and to his family more than thirty years ago. Raya would go and visit him, at first with her mother, and, after her marriage, with Yehuda. What bothered them was that they were compelled to listen to his talk about Mendele his grandson, and to read that same lament for his native town which had been destroyed.

Whenever Rachel happened to come here during their visit, she would scold Grandfather rudely. "Stop bothering them with your masterpiece," she would say, and herself remove the papers from the table and put them back in their bag. "If you want them to keep on visiting you, don't talk to them about the dead. Talk about the living. They're young people and they have no mind for such things."

And as they left his room together she would say, turning to Yehuda in order to placate him, "Don't be surprised at him. Grandfather's already old. Over seventy. Loss of memory."

When Raya was seven months pregnant, Grandfather Zisskind had in his absent-mindedness not yet noticed it. But Rachel could no longer refrain from letting him share her joy and hope, and told him that a great-grandchild would soon be born to him. One evening the door of Raya and Yehuda's flat opened, and Grandfather himself stood on the threshold in his holiday clothes, just as on the day of Mendele's birthday. This was the first time he had visited them at home, and Raya was so surprised that she hugged and kissed him as she had not done since she was a child. His face shone, his eyes sparkled with the same intelligent and mischievous light they had in those far-off days before the calamity. When he entered he walked briskly through the rooms, giving his opinion on the furniture and its arrangement, and joking about everything around him. He was so pleasant that Raya and Yehuda could not stop laughing all the time he was speaking. He gave no indication that he knew what was about to take place, and for the first time in many months he did not mention Mendele.

"Ah, you naughty children," he said, "is this how you treat Grandfather? Why didn't you tell me you had such a nice place?"

"How many times have I invited you here, Grandfather?" asked Raya.

"Invited me? You ought to have *brought* me here, dragged me by force!"

"I wanted to do that too, but you refused."

"Well, I thought that you lived in some dark den, and I have a den of my own. Never mind, I forgive you."

And when he took leave of them he said:

"Don't bother to come to me. Now that I know where you're to be found and what a palace you have, I'll come to you...if you don't throw me out, that is."

Some days later, when Rachel came to their home and they told her about Grandfather's amazing visit, she was not surprised:

"Ah, you don't know what he's been contemplating during all

these days, ever since I told him that you're about to have a child...He has one wish—that if it's a son, it should be named...after his grandson."

"Mendele?" exclaimed Raya, and involuntarily burst into laughter. Yehuda smiled as one smiles at the fond fancies of the old.

"Of course, I told him to put that out of his head," said Rachel, "but you know how obstinate he is. It's some obsession and he won't think of giving it up. Not only that, but he's sure that you'll willingly agree to it, and especially you, Yehuda."

Yehuda shrugged his shoulders. "Crazy. The child would be unhappy all his life."

"But he's not capable of understanding that," said Rachel, and a note of apprehension crept into her voice.

Raya's face grew solemn. "We have already decided on the name," she said. "If it's a girl she'll be called Osnath, and if it's a boy—Ehud."

Rachel did not like either.

The matter of the name became almost the sole topic of conversation between Rachel and the young couple when she visited them, and it infused gloom into the air of expectancy which filled the house.

Rachel, midway between the generations, was of two minds about the matter. When she spoke to her father she would scold and contradict him, flinging at him all the arguments she had heard from Raya and Yehuda as though they were her own, but when she spoke to the children she sought to induce them to meet his wishes, and would bring down their anger on herself. As time went on, the question of a name, to which in the beginning she had attached little importance, became a kind of mystery, concealing something preordained , fearful, and pregnant with life and death. The fate of the child itself seemed in doubt. In her innermost heart she prayed that Raya would give birth to a daughter.

"Actually, what's so bad about the name Mendele?" she asked her daughter. "It's a Jewish name like any other."

"What are you talking about, Mother"—Raya rebelled against the thought—"a Ghetto name, ugly, horrible! I wouldn't even be capable of letting it cross my lips. Do you want me to hate my child?"

"Oh, you won't hate your child. At any rate, not because of the name..."

"I should hate him. It's as if you'd told me that my child would be born with a hump! And anyway—why should I? What for?"

"You have to do it for Grandfather's sake," Rachel said quietly, although she knew that she was not speaking the whole truth.

"You know, Mother, that I am ready to do anything for Grandfather," said Raya. "I love him, but I am not ready to sacrifice my child's happiness on account of some superstition of his. What sense is there in it?"

Rachel could not explain the "sense in it" rationally, but in her heart she rebelled against her daughter's logic which had always been hers too and now seemed very superficial, a symptom of the frivolity afflicting the younger generation. Her old father now appeared to her like an ancient tree whose deep roots suck up the mysterious essence of existence, of which neither her daughter nor she herself knew anything. Had it not been for this argument about the name, she would certainly never have got to meditating on the transmigration of souls and the eternity of life. At night she would wake up covered in cold sweat. Hazily, she recalled frightful scenes of bodies of naked children, beaten and trampled under the jackboots of soldiers, and an awful sense of guilt oppressed her spirit.

Then Rachel came with a proposal for a compromise: that the child should be named Menachem. A Hebrew name, she said; an Israeli one, by all standards. Many children bore it, and it occurred to nobody to make fun of them. Even Grandfather had agreed to it after much urging.

Raya refused to listen.

"We have chosen a name, Mother," she said, "which we both like, and we won't change it for another. Menachem is a name which reeks of old age, a name which for me is connected with sad memories and people I don't like. Menachem you could call only a boy who is short, weak and not good-looking. Let's not talk about it any more, Mother."

Rachel was silent. She almost despaired of convincing them. At last she said:

"And are you ready to take the responsibility of going against Grandfather's wishes?"

Raya's eyes opened wide, and fear was reflected in them:

"Why do you make such a fateful thing of it? You frighten me!" she said, and burst into tears. She began to fear for her offspring as one fears the evil eye.

"And perhaps there is something fateful in it..." whispered Rachel without raising her eyes. She flinched at her own words.

"What is it?" insisted Raya, with a frightened look at her mother.

"I don't know..." she said. "Perhaps all the same we are bound to retain the names of the dead...in order to leave a rememberance of them..." She was not sure herself whether there was any truth in what she said or whether it was merely a stupid belief, but her father's faith was before her, stronger than her own doubts and her daughter's simple and understandable opposition.

"But I don't always want to remember all those dreadful things, Mother. It's impossible that this memory should always hang about this house and that the poor child should bear it!"

Rachel understood. She, too, heard such a cry within her as she listened to her father talking, sunk in memories of the past. As if to herself, she said in a whisper:

"I don't know...at times it seems to me that it's not Grandfather who's suffering from loss of memory, but ourselves. All of us."

About two weeks before the birth was due, Grandfather Zisskind appeared in Raya and Yehuda's home for the second time. His face was yellow, angry, and the light had faded from his eyes. He greeted them, but did not favor Raya with so much as a glance, as if he had pronounced a ban upon the sinner. Turning to Yehuda he said, "I wish to speak to you."

They went into the inner room. Grandfather sat down on the chair and placed the palm of his hand on the edge of the table, as was his wont, and Yehuda sat, lower than he, on the bed.

"Rachel has told me that you don't want to call the child by my grandchild's name," he said.

"Yes..." said Yehuda diffidently.

"Perhaps you'll explain to me why?" he asked.

"We..." stammered Yehuda, who found it difficult to face the piercing gaze of the old man. "The name simply doesn't appeal to us."

Grandfather was silent. Then he said, "I understand that Mendele doesn't appeal to you. Not a Hebrew name. Granted! But Menachem—what's wrong with Menachem?" It was obvious that he was controlling his feelings with difficulty.

"It's not..." Yehuda knew that there was no use explaining; they were two generations apart in their ideas. "It's not an Israeli name...it's from the *Golah (Diaspora)."*

"Golah," repeated Grandfather. He shook with rage, but somehow he maintained his self-control. Quietly he added, "We all come from the *Golah.* I, and Raya's father and mother. Your father and mother. All of us."

"Yes..." said Yehuda. He resented the fact that he was being dragged into an argument which was distasteful to him, particularly with this old man whose mind was already not quite clear. Only out of respect did he restrain himself from shouting: That's that, and it's done with!..."Yes, but we were born in this country," he said aloud; "that's different."

Grandfather Zisskind looked at him contemptuously. Before him he saw a wretched boor, an empty vessel.

"You, that is to say, think that there's something new here," he said, "that everything that was there is past and gone. Dead, without sequel. That you are starting everything anew."

"I didn't say that. I only said that we were born in this country..."

"You were born here. Very nice..." said Grandfather Zisskind with rising emotion. "So what of it? What's so remarkable about that? In what way are you superior to those who were born *there?* Are you cleverer than they? More cultured? Are you greater than they in Torah or good deeds? Is your blood redder than theirs? Grandfather Zisskind looked as if he could wring Yehuda's neck.

"I didn't say that either. I said that *here* it's different..."

Grandfather Zisskind's patience with idle words was exhausted.

"You good-for-nothing!" he burst out in his rage. "What do you know about what was there? What do you know of the *people* that were there? The communities? The cities? What do you know of the *life* they had there?"

"Yes," said Yehuda, his spirit crushed, "but we no longer have any ties with it."

"You have no ties with it?" Grandfather Zisskind bent towards him. His lips quivered in fury. "With what...with what *do* you have ties?"

"We have...with this country," said Yehuda and gave an involuntary smile.

"Fool!" Grandfather Zisskind shot at him. "Do you think that people come to a desert and make themselves a nation, eh? That you are the first of some new race? That you're not the son of your father? Not the grandson of your grandfather? Do you want to forget them? Are you ashamed of them for having had a hundred times more culture and education than you have? Why...why, everything here"—he included everything around him in the sweep of his arm— "is no more than a puddle of tapwater against the big sea that was there! What have you here? A mixed multitude! Seventy languages! Seventy distinct groups! Customs? A way of life? Why, every home here is a nation in itself, with its own customs and its own names! And with this you have ties, you say..."

Yehuda lowered his eyes and was silent.

"I'll tell you what ties are," said Grandfather Zisskind calmly. "Ties are remembrance! Do you understand? The Russian is linked to his people because he remembers his ancestors. He is called Ivan, his father was called Ivan and his grandfather was called Ivan, back to the first generation. And no Russian has said: From today onwards I shall not be called Ivan because my fathers and my fathers' fathers were called that; I am the first of a new Russian nation which has nothing at all to do with the Ivans. Do you understand?"

"But what has that got to do with it?" Yehuda protested impatiently. Grandfather Zisskind shook his head at him.

"And you—you're ashamed to give your son the name Mendele lest it remind you that there were Jews who were called by that name. You believe that his name should be wiped off the face of the earth. That not a trace of it should remain..."

He paused, heaved a deep sigh and said:

"O children, children, you don't know what you're doing...You're finishing off the work which the enemies of Israel began. They took the bodies away from the world, and you—the name and the memory...No continuation, no evidence, no memorial and no name. Not a trace..."

And with that he rose, took his stick and with long strides went towards the door and left.

The newborn child was a boy and he was named Ehud, and when he was about a month old, Raya and Yehuda took him in the carriage to Grandfather's house.

Raya gave three cautious knocks on the door, and when she heard a rustle inside she could also hear the beating of her anxious heart. Since the birth of the child Grandfather had not visited them even once. "I'm terribly excited," she whispered to Yehuda with tears in her eyes. Yehuda rocked the carriage and did not reply. He was now indifferent to what the old man might say or do.

The door opened, and on the threshold stood Grandfather Zisskind, his face weary and wrinkled. He seemed to have aged. His eyes were sticky with sleep, and for a moment it seemed as if he did not see the callers.

"Good Sabbath, Grandfather," said Raya with great feeling. It seemed to her now that she loved him more than ever.

Grandfather looked at them as if surprised, and then said absently, "Come in, come in."

"We've brought the baby with us!" said Raya, her face shining, and her glance traveled from Grandfather to the infant sleeping in the carriage.

"Come in, come in," repeated Grandfather Zisskind in a tired voice. "Sit down," he said as he removed his clothes from the chairs and turned to tidy the disordered bedclothes.

Yehuda stood the carriage by the wall and whispered to Raya, "It's stifling for him here." Raya opened the window wide.

"You haven't seen our baby yet, Grandfather!" she said with a sad smile.

"Sit down, sit down," said Grandfather, shuffling over to the shelf, from which he took the jar of preserves and the biscuit tin, putting them on the table.

"There's no need, Grandfather, really there's no need for it. We didn't come for that," said Raya.

"Only a little something. I have nothing to offer you today..." said Grandfather in a dull, broken voice. He took the kettle off the kerosene burner and poured out two glasses of tea which he placed before them. Then he too sat down, said, "Drink, drink," and softly tapped his fingers on the table.

"I haven't seen Mother for several days now," he said at last.

"She's busy..." said Raya in a low voice, without raising her eyes to him. "She helps me a lot with the baby..."

Grandfather Zisskind looked at his pale, knotted and veined hands lying helplessly on the table; then he stretched out one of them and said to Raya, "Why don't you drink? The tea will get cold."

Raya drew up to the table and sipped the tea.

"And you—what are you doing now?" he asked Yehuda.

"Working as usual," said Yehuda, and added with a laugh, "I play with the baby when there's time."

Grandfather again looked down at his hands, the long thin fingers of which shook with the palsy of old age.

"Take some of the preserves," he said to Yehuda, indicating the jar with a shaking finger. "It's very good." Yehuda dipped the spoon in the jar and put it to his mouth.

There was a deep silence. It seemed to last a very long time. Grandfather Zisskind's fingers gave little quivers on the white tablecloth. It was hot in the room, and the buzzing of a fly could be heard.

Suddenly the baby burst out crying, and Raya started from her seat and hastened to quiet him. She rocked the carriage and crooned, "Quiet, child, quiet, quiet..." Even after he had quieted down she went on rocking the carriage back and forth.

Grandfather Zisskind raised his head and said to Yehuda in a whisper:

"You think it was impossible to save him...it was possible. They had many friends. Ossip himself wrote to me about it. The manager of the factory had a high opinion of him. The whole town knew them and loved them...How is it they didn't think of it...?" he said, touching his forehead with the palm of his hand. "After all, they knew that the Germans were approaching...It was still possible to do something..."

He stopped a moment and then added, "Imagine that a boy of eleven had already finished his studies at the Conservatory—wild beasts!" He suddenly opened his eyes filled with terror. "Wild beasts! To take little children and put them into wagons and deport them..."

When Raya returned and sat down at the table, he stopped and became silent, and only a heavy sigh escaped from deep within him.

Again there was a prolonged silence, and as it grew heavier Raya felt the oppresive weight on her bosom increasing till it could no longer be contained. Grandfather sat at the table tapping his thin fingers, and alongside the wall the infant lay in his carriage; it was as if a chasm gaped between a world which was passing and a world that was born. It was no longer a single line to the fourth generation. The aged father did not recognize the great-grandchild whose life would be no memorial.

Grandfather Zisskind got up, took his chair and pulled it up to the clock. He climbed on to it to take out his documents.

Raya could no longer stand the oppressive atmosphere.

"Let's go," she said to Yehuda in a choked voice.

"Yes, we must go," said Yehuda, and rose from his seat. "We have to go," he said loudly as he turned to the old man.

Grandfather Zisskind held the key of the clock for a moment more, then he let his hand fall, grasped the back of the chair and got down.

"You have to go..." he said with a tortured grimace. He spread his arms out helplessly and accompanied them to the doorway.

When the door had closed behind them the tears flowed from Raya's eyes. She bent over the carriage and pressed her lips to the baby's chest. At that moment it seemed to her that he was in need of pity and of great love, as though he were alone, an orphan in the world.

Since 1950 Aharon Megged has worked as editor of the weekly literary supplement of Lamerhav in Tel Aviv. He is known as a short story writer and playwright. The story was translated by Minna Givton.

"What do you care? They think their father is dead."

A Short Visit

BY YUKIKO HIROTA

WHEN I entered the kitchen from the back door, I saw the back of a man sitting on the floor and eating. He was big, robust. I instinctively grabbed at a log by the door. Then, instantly I relaxed. The way he ate . . . No one ate that way except my brother-in-law. Or my ex-brother-in-law? He didn't even bother to sit at the table. He sat by the cabinet where the rice and soup bowls were kept. He always ate that way. As if he were trying to set a new speed record in an eating race!

"Burglar!" I shouted, holding up the log in the air.

The man jumped up, turned around and said, "It's me!"

"Who are you? You're stealing our rice!" I shouted again.

"Oh, come on! I was so hungry, I came home to eat!"

"Came home!" I scoffed, placing the log down by my side. "Where have you been all these years? For over two years! No word!"

"Where are the girls?"

"What do you care? They think their father is dead. You're not their father! No father just leaves his babies for more than two years! All you do is gamble and drink! This is not your home!"

He hastened his eating.

"You'd better disappear right away. My father will kill you if he sees you. He thinks you killed my sister. I think so, too! You neglected her during all her married life. You never worked to support her. We always supported you and your family . . . How could you come back like this? To fill your stomach! I'm telling you he'll kill you!"

I knew my father would, at least, try to hit him with the log or something. This man was in his late twenties. Though my father was big, he was already in his mid-fifties and he would lose if a fight started.

"You take care of my babies," the man stood up, still biting a pickle.

I was shaking in anger. "Get out!" I shouted. Then, I saw my father coming.

My brother-in-law saw my despairing look and said, "What's the matter?" He turned his head to face my father.

"What's he doing here in my house, Asako?" my father shouted at me.

"He was eating when I came in," I replied.

"Hungry beggar! Get out of my house!" my father shouted without looking at him.

"I'm your son-in-law!" the younger man shouted.

"I don't have a son-in-law!" my father roared.

"Oh, my God!" the younger man groaned.

At least they weren't using their hands in fighting. I had to get the man out before a real fight began.

"Burglar! Rice thief! Get out!" I shouted.

The younger man rushed out with no more word. I heaved a sigh. My father sat down at the table. I was glad the twin girls were out now. I had persuaded my mother to take them to the special show for children which was put on by the kindergarten children in the city park.

"I have to cook rice again because he has eaten the whole thing!

The way he ate! You remember the way he used to eat? The same way!" I said, sighing.

"Don't talk about him. It makes me sick!" my father said.

I didn't blame him. My younger sister Harue Shimoda and Goro Kato were married when she was sixteen and Goro was twenty. My sister was always a weak girl and Goro was such a big strong boy that my parents were sure he would take good care of her. Goro was from a farm outside our city. He and Harue lived in our house. Harue had twins three years later. During the first three years of their marriage, Goro changed jobs more than five times and was out of work in between. He didn't like farming which my father did. When the twin girls were two years old, my sister died of acute pneumonia. Goro had left our house a few months before that, telling us he was going to get a job in Tokyo. I took charge of my sister's children. About half a year after Harue's death, Goro came back penniless. He stayed in our house for a while. Before his children got used to him, he left us again without telling us anything.

The twin girls were now five years old. They were like my own children to me. Even when my sister was alive, she was so weak that I had to take care of them most of the time. I would have to make plans seriously. . . . My parents would be too old soon . . . I'd be the only person the girls could turn to—unless, of course, Goro miraculously would turn into a reliable person in time. It would be foolish to count on that—wishful thinking. I'd have to get a job and support my nieces. Maybe, I should legally adopt them . . . but Goro could be in the way. I didn't expect myself to get married . . . I was already in mid-thirties . . . I had never thought of getting married . . . I had always been taking care of my sister . . .

By the time dinner was ready, my mother and the twin girls had come back. They were excitedly chatting about the show they had seen. My mother immediately noticed my father's dangerous mood and occasionally tossed an inquiring look at me, but I ignored it. Rather, I concentrated on enjoying the girls' chatting. I didn't want to mention Goro in front of the girls.

After dinner the girls were tired. They were tiny for their age and weren't too strong. I put them to bed and then my father and I told my mother about Goro. My mother sighed. We all sighed. Goro was still young. He would come back *home* often as long as he was alive. And his children should know the facts. It was true, in a sense, that their father was dead . . . Goro had sent us no word for more than two years. He had been away before that, too! So, it was also true that the girls had had no father . . .

"He doesn't care about his children! He said to me, 'You take care of my babies.' And that in between bites! He doesn't even want to see his own children! He just doesn't care! I can't believe Harue was so stupid as to marry that man!" I fumed.

"Well, she was stupid, I guess. We were stupid, too. I'm going to bed," my father said, sounding defeated.

My mother was tired, too, after being out all afternoon with the twins, and went to bed soon. I was still too upset to go to bed. Then, I heard some knocks on the back door. I went to the door and saw Goro through the glass section of the door.

"What do you want now?" I whispered in a sharp tone.

"Let me take a look at the girls. Then, I'll leave right away. Promise!" he also whispered.

So, he wanted to see his children at least . . . I was glad to know that. Harue should be happy, too . . . I opened the door and said, "Don't wake them."

While he watched the girls sleeping side by side, I examined his clothes. They were dirty and ragged. He was still wearing winter clothes. Now everyone was wearing light between-spring-and-summer clothes.

"Thanks," Goro said meekly.

"Are you hungry again?" I said.

"No," he mumbled sheepishly.

"Do you have money?"

"No."

I went to my room and brought my handbag. I emptied my wallet and gave him the whole thing. I had no idea how much I had in my wallet. Goro took it silently, turned around and left. Watching him disappear in the dark, I slowly locked the door. I told myself I had just made a grave mistake. That's why he'd come back again and again! I was too kind, I felt chagrined. I scolded myself. I should be so mean that he would be afraid to come back! But then, he was my sister's husband and her children's father . . .

Yukiko Hirota is the pen-name of Hisako Hasegawa. Born in Japan in 1934, she has been writing since her teens. She is fluent in Japanese and English. Hisako Hasegawa perfected her English working at an American Army base in Japan. Her most recent stories are written in English. She is presently in the USA.

" 'Reverend,' he began, 'if you will permit me, I must raise a little matter before we cast our vote.' "

By Acclamation

BY FRANCIS EBEJER

THROUGH the wishy-washy light of early evening, Giomarija was riding his donkey sidesaddle from the few fig trees on his rocky patrimonial patch upon the Hill of The Three Flutes back to the village, when the animal slithered to a groggy halt just outside Lukrezja's wineshop and refused to budge any farther.

Unknown then to anybody else but the gods (and, of course, the writer of this extraordinary piece of Mediterranean mayhem) the donkey's reactionary gesture signaled the start of a procession of events to lead Giomarija—long, gaunt, sixty-seven and sexton—to a position of no mean influence in the village.

After several unsuccessful attempts—some unwittingly borrowed from the field of aerodynamics—to restart the donkey, he threw his arms up to clutch the mellow air, stalked over on—he could have sworn—his knees to Lukrezja's shop and, once there, ordered wine for himself and for the three or four samaritans who had labored with brawn, if not with any unseemly extravagance of brain, against the donkey's obduracy.

Then, settling his bony back hurtfully against an empty olive barrel, on top of which an assortment of cakes, buns and *kannoli* left over from the annual festa, fought, inside a glass case, a losing battle with half a slab of sheep's cheese, Giomarija proceeded to wash down with wine his dither over the donkey.

But, as has already been pointed out, the donkey was only the beginning: two large ears and four somewhat aged legs engagingly signposting a dubious future.

For, even while he was seriously contemplating a possible successor to his tenth replenishment, in between thinking quite untoward thoughts about his wretch of an animal, there came to Giomarija's ears the tintinnabulation of the tiniest bell in the church belfry.

All at once, the ends of his thoroughly unkempt moustache began a rotary movement with a distinctly ominous anti-clockwise bent, his thick eyebrows shot up and over the low ceiling of his forehead and, uttering an expletive-filigreed howl of some chagrin, he stumbled out into the street.

The first thing that Giomarija noticed was an excruciatingly empty space where his donkey should have been; and the second, that the bell was being rung in a manner that would have broken the hearts of not one but a thousand village sextons, all expertly self-trained in riotous cacophony.

"I'm indeed a hapless man," he exclaimed in the general direction of fat, buxom Lukrezja and the others, not forgetting to apportion a few cutting glances upwards where he imagined the gods to be sitting—namely, upon, he fervently hoped, the bumpier bits of the cirrocumulus clouds which at that moment were canopying the village. "My donkey has walked out on me; and someone who indubitably is not myself is ringing the bell. Tell me, am I my donkey's keeper or am I not? And am I the sacristan of this village or am I not?"

His first question was answered when, having, in a manner of speaking, run to the church, he found his donkey contentedly licking away at the scaling limestone—an asses' delicacy—of the belfry tower. The answer to his second query was provided for him by Dun

Manwel himself who descended upon him in a swirl of generous soutane.

"So!" intoned Dun Manwel, pointing a finger of wrath at his sexton. "Here at last is our excellent church curator back from his leisurely peregrinations. I wonder what excuse he has ready for me this time. For the third time this week, the hour of evening service and benediction arrives, and where is our sexton? I may well ask myself. Alas, he is nowhere to be seen, I may well reply. Alas, he does no longer exist. Alas, poor Giomarija has been trundled off, at long last, by a brigade of nether spirits. And it is left for me, as if I have no more important things to see to, to ring the confounded, er, bell myself. I warned you last time, Giomarija, that I would not tolerate a repetition, and this time indeed I will not."

"It was my donkey, Reverence..." began Giomarija with a bravura that would have brought tears to a judge's eyes.

"A likely story!" retorted Dun Manwel, who had never graced the precincts of a Court of Law. "Much against my will, I have arrived back at the foregone conclusion, however tortuously, that you are nothing but a wastrel of a sexton. And I have nothing more to say to you." And, with that, Dun Manwel strode off to disappear inside the church.

Feeling desolate and perturbed inside a wine-hued mist, Giomarija first allowed his moustache to droop to a suitably despondent level and then began to count his misfortunes on his fingers. Exactly on the fourth, fate made itself evident once more—as if one of the cirrocumulus gods had slipped rather heavily off the bumpy seat onto which Giomarija had earlier relegated him.

Giomarija heard his name called. Turning around, he saw none other than Sur Benin Attard who was standing right at the bottom of the church steps, busy beckoning him with a multiple-ringed finger.

"You want me?" an agape Giomarija managed to utter.

"My woebegone man," began Sur Benin when he finally had Giomarija by his side, "I harbor a strange suspicion that I have arrived just in time to save you from a fate worse than the stake." Then, dropping his voice to a conspiratorial whisper, he added: "But come, Giomarija. For reasons with which I shall acquaint you by-and-by, it will not do for us to be seen keeping each other company.

So, be a good man, drag your donkey home, and afterwards rendezvous with me, won't you, at the village gate, just outside the old Grandmaster's archway, where I shall be waiting for you in my car. You can't miss it as I'm sure you haven't seen anything like it."

And so it was that half an hour later, Sur Benin, redolent of hair lotion, was driving Giomarija in his Alphasud towards the Villa Attard, a matter of a kilometer and a half away from the village.

"What a fortunate moment in my life!" he was saying later to Giomarija who was barely sitting on the edge of a spacious armchair flanked on each side by an enormous Apuli vase with artificial zinnias and one live arum lily. "What a fortunate moment it was for me to come upon your gracious person just when I did and under such propitious circumstances." And before Giomarija, goggle-eyed and dumb, could begin to unravel what propitiousness could have possibly lain in his tiff with Dun Manwel, Sur Benin came forward with decanter and glass.

"You will drink this, Giomarija, my friend, will you not?" he invited. "There is nothing like a draught of undoctored grape wine—such a rarity, as I know you will concur—to rouse oneself from thoughts of despair and self-annihilation."

"I shall never forgive myself, never!" Giomarija exclaimed weepily, taking the wine and proceeding at once to spill some of it over his trousers—very much in the manner, one is tempted to point out, of a libation, however unconscious and perhaps just that little bit too late, to the unquiet gods.

"But you must desist from even talking like that, my good friend," interrupted the other. "You're as blameless as a newly born babe. Tell me, does an infant ever soil itself for the willful pleasure of despoiling another of darling mamma's little nappies? No, of course not. On the other hand, it is well known, is it not, that our excellent parish priest does so often permit the wrong ideas to inflate his poor, little head. It is a failing with him. Tell me, dear friend, how long have you been honoring the village in the enviable capacity of a sexton?"

"Nigh on forty years, sinjur, no less."

"So! And now, after all that period of time during which only God knows what you've been up to, you are sent away, cast off from the sight of the righteous, and without the slightest valediction. You find yourself without honest employ. Believe me, I commiserate with you most deeply. My friend, I weep for you." Upon which, Sur Benin sniffed twice.

Giomarija stirred uneasily in his chair, which ominously had began to recede from the little of him that was still on it. "I do not think that I have lost my employ, your worship, sir," he remarked. "He did not say so."

"Ah, but forgive me, he did say so."

"He did?"

"Most emphatically, yes. Was I not there to hear him, and did not my heart bleed—there it goes again!—on your behalf? He said: 'You are a wastrel of a sexton. You're an ignorant and irresponsible one; an inefficient, time-wasting buffoon. Never will I tolerate a sacristan such as you. Get hence from my sight. Buffoon!' Isn't that precisely how the good Dun Manwel accorded himself the unique pleasure of addressing you?"

"I believe so," replied Giomarija weakly, emptying his glass which Sur Benin refilled at once.

Having reached this plane of intellectual understanding, the two men continued with their dialogue which, jollified with a rapid succession of draughts of wine and replete with metaphysical references to Dun Manwel and his inexplicable way of not doing the right things, ranged far into the brooding, fateful night...

The new Giomarija that appeared in the village streets the following morning brought people rushing out of their houses. They had never seen anything like it! Sitting on Giomarija's head was a fedora hat which, though on the large side, yet slanted over his right eye to near-blinding effect, while the faint but unmistakable whiffs of hair lotion which still adhered to it only served to enhance its urbane quality.

The trousers of white serge were more than a trifle baggy at the back, and short at the ankles, revealing a sizable sockless area above the creaking patent shoes, but no one could gainsay that the creases down the legs were all that a hysterically geometrical mind could devise. The tie he was wearing was long and broad enough to allow the two palm trees depicted on it to sway to a singularly sartorial breeze.

He had trimmed his moustache to two fine points, most obviously and recently waxed. Between his surviving teeth reposed a cigar of opulent dimensions, while over the rim of the breast pocket of the white jacket, the doubtlessly expensive brand of another flashed unashamedly in full view of everyone.

When the people gathered around wanting to touch him, as they would a hand-blackened foot of a papier-mâché saint, Giomarija soon gave evidence of being a thing alive through the simple expertise of flicking the ash from his cigar upon their inquisitive fingers and calling them either uneducated, ignorant oafs or, more frequently, and quite inventively, buffoons.

Not that he played the lord, too given to exclusivity, to extremes. On the contrary, there were long moments, especially in the evenings at Lukrezja's popular establishment, when he seemed to delight in having the greatest possible number of people pressing around and happily treading on one another's corns just for the sheer pleasure of seeing him and hearing him talk.

And this new Giomarija, once he started, never seemed to stop; and strange and wildly disturbing were the things that he had to recount.

He would start with the matter of the church pulpit and the odious woodworms which were slowly devouring it; he would draw a graphic description of the deteriorating state of the painting behind the main altar; and usually finish up by thundering forth that the damask hangings, which were used for the main festa in the liturgical calendar, had been badly needing a few well-placed stitches for the last twenty years, or possibly even more unto who knows what God-forsaken generations back!

"Mind you," he continued quite darkly one evening, "I did my best as a good and dutiful parishioner, for many were the times when I drew the attention of our much respected pastor to this lamentable state of affairs. But, alas, he would give me one senile reply after another, all to the visible effect that there was no money, and that things must wait. Which means, I presume, that we must all wait until the pulpit, with him on it, finally collapses about our ears; the hangings fall into shreds over our heads; and the titular painting of the celebrated Calabrese—Caravaggio, no less—becomes bare, damp wall again before our very eyes." He raised one gnarled, prophecy-stanced finger towards Lukrezja's overworked fly-catchers. *"He* says there is *no* money." He paused. "But I, one Giomarija by name, man of substance and great inside knowledge, do hereby tell *you* that there *is."*

"The *kappillan* is right, there's no money," broke in a small, bald man in a piping voice, hoping he was safely lost in the crowd.

Nothing, however, seemed to be lost on Giomarija. Removing the cigar from his mouth with deliberate, tension-loaded slowness, swiftly decapitating it and, at the same instance, exhibiting great thoughtfulness in ensuring that the severed ash dropped straight into one of Lukrezja's clay bowls in which she kept chopped-up sardines, and not on the floor, he crossed over to the importunate heckler.

"So!" he said, his face close to the other's. "You aver that the priest is right, and that there is no money!"

"I so aver," responded the other, trying to gain an inch, but soon falling back on his heels with the one intent to vanish.

"Imbecile! Have you not forgotten one little detail? What say you to the money he has been collecting from us over these many Sundays after the eight o'clock Mass? What about that money, I venture to ask you?"

This seemed to imply to the people such a glaring misconception that they all spoke up at once. "But you know as well as we do, Giomarija, that that money is for the communal farm."

"Ah!" exclaimed Giomarija, flourishing his cigar and dispensing more ash, quite unintentionally, of course, over the head of the small, bald man. "I was expecting such a comment, such a referendum. You say it is for the farm. And it is true...you are not liars...only stupid! It is for the farm, yes, but..." He stopped, emptied his mug, wiped his lips and moustache with the aid of Lukrezja's ample apron, and resumed: "But if it is truly for the farm, then are we not all as good as dry sticks ready to be thrust into eternal fire?"

Allowing the assembled citizenry sufficient time for a long gasp and at least one corporate wary glance at a couple of, no doubt, demon-infested cracks in Lukrezja's walls, he went on: "Here we are, throwing our cents into Dun Manwel's collection bag, and for what purpose, may I ask you? To amend the scandalous condition of our small church?"

"Oh, it's not all that bad," came the voice of the presumptuous little man again, his bald pate giving a semblance of miraculously grown hair where he had smudged ash from Giomarija's cigar.

This time, however, Giomarija chose to ignore the less-than-nothing, instantly redressing the balance by putting on a deeply pained look.

"Is it for that?" he rhetoricized, breaking up his voice into a sob or two behind a huge bandana which he had unfurled from an inside pocket. "No, of course not. Then for what? For what indeed but to build this farm so that we might debauch ourselves with food, which, whatever certain cretinous others say to the contrary, would not be cheaper than that procurable on the normal market, let me assure you. And while we are wallowing in thoughts of the farm, of our miserable, perishable bodies even"—pausing slightly to straighten his tie and adjust his hat at a vainer angle—"we neglect God's own house...Friends, I prophesy that nothing but fire and brimstone will be our lot if we proceed with this evil business that goes under the beguiling name of...communal farm. It has always been a matter of surprise to me that the *kappillan* himself should have been the first one to think of this infernal scheme. Surely, he is not so blind, not completely such a...*buffoon,* as not to be aware of the state of the pulpit, and of the damask hangings, and of the titular painting..."

Giomarija's crusading spirit had been inflaming the minds of the villagers for some time before Dun Manwel began to notice its effects in the form of very poor collections on at least three consecutive Sundays.

It must be said for Dun Manwel that he had been secretly pleased at seeing Giomarija evidently doing so well for himself, for he had long regretted his outburst with him; and yet he could not really understand why Giomarija should have taken it so much to heart: they had had altercations before. He had even been not a little amused when they had come up to tell him about Giomarija's wild talk in the village, which Dun Manwel had at once and good-humoredly put down as the expression of an aging midwife's puny desire to belabor him in the interest of face-saving.

But this was serious. Never on the many Sundays of collections for the communal farm had he netted such paltry sums.

He recalled with what joy the people had greeted his idea of a collective enterprise for the village; so much so that the farmers, largely smallholders in those parts, had immediately promised their cooperation.

He and his Civic Committee had spared no efforts in explaining the aims of the project. First, the instilling of a civic and cooperative spirit; secondly, reasonable and exclusive prices for the village folk; and then, no less important, the laying aside of part of the profits to enable them, not merely to patch up the church where it needed patching up, but, ultimately, to overhaul it completely, indeed to make it the fairest church in the whole district.

Now the whole plan faced ruin.

Dun Manwel knitted his brows, with four fingers engineered a diamond shape under his chin, and pondered. Sadness filled his heart. Things were even coming to such a pass that several of his flock had begun to turn off into all kinds and manner of side streets, after hailing non-existent friends and acquaintances, whenever they saw him approaching.

He sipped his Nigret, a wine normally so dear to his heart but now tasting more like bicarbonate soda, and continued to ponder until he reached a point when he felt he should act more and ponder less.

He started convening the Committee more frequently. From the pulpit, precarious a perch though it was—Giomarija had been right about the industrious woodworms busy at their perforations—he expounded again and again on the merits of the farm plan, hoping to rekindle the people's enthusiasm and their faith in him.

He spoke to the women at the countless gossip points around the village, and to the men on the church-square, when they were sober; when they were not, outside the wineshop, in those few precious seconds when fresh air seemed to break through their befuddlement for the first and last time.

It all seemed to be in vain. The collections continued to dwindle, and he could almost hear the people remarking as he passed: "God's House first and foremost!" Which made him feel mildly sacrilegious and intensely angry and uncharitable towards that moldy ass of a

Giomarija!

One night, however, after a lengthy prayer session at his *prie-dieu,* the first suspicion crossed his mind. He lost no time early next morning in calling to him some of his more trusted confidants and bidding them to watch and take note.

He was surprised at the thoroughness of their work. They unanimously reported seeing Giomarija tiptoeing forth in the dark, at least three times a week, in the direction of a certain villa...the sound of at least two men roistering till the early hours behind the shuttered windows of the said villa...a Giomarija lording it among the servants of, again, the said villa...

No one could have desired more direct evidence!

But Dun Manwel, being the way he was, was ready to discount his worst suspicions had it not been that, one day, on emerging from the Archiepiscopal Palace at Valletta, whither he was wont to repair once a month, his eyes happened to alight on a car lessening speed to allow a horse-cab to negotiate a difficult corner. He had at once recognized Sur Benin Attard at the wheel. Seated next to him was Giomarija with his now inevitable cigar, ostentatious band and all, while, in the back, sat a corpulent personage whom Dun Manwel knew to be a big noise in the vegetable brokerage business in the Rabat and Pwales areas.

"It is obvious," Dun Manwel told his Committee that very same evening, "that Sur Benin and his city business friends may be viewing this communal farm of ours as not being in their best interests. As most of the farmers would be in the cooperative plan, these gentlemen might even be thinking that they are being robbed of a very cheap market. They have nearly all the Maltese Islands to do business in, and yet they would not even tolerate an exception in such a tiny village as ours."

"So all this talk," said the schoolmaster, "about the renovation of the church coming first is, of course, to..."

"Make us kiss the farm good-bye," broke in the church organist, who had, in the mid-Twenties, been as far afield as Long Island, U.S.A., and had now momentarily lapsed into the language of that country—a normal practice among former exiles easily prone to great emotion. "They're trying to twist our arms into scrapping the whole idea by screwing up the people against it and hooking them with this renovation hoo-ey."

"That is precisely what I fear to be the case," dolefully remarked Dun Manwel, not really comprehending the other. "Sur Benin and Giomarija seem to have worked it well between them, have they not? Only the Almighty can help us now." And that night he felt he must pray harder than ever, meanwhile taking conscientious care not to wish the belfry tower, and other allied discomforts, to fall too heavily upon his ex-sexton's head.

Next morning, immediately after Mass, he was surprised to find no less an unwished-for personage than Sur Benin Attard himself waiting for him in the vestry.

"It rejoices my heart to honor you with my visit," said Sur Benin slyly. He was already relaxing in a worn leather chair which was almost as ancient as the church itself, if slightly safer. Dun Manwel eyed him suspiciously.

The Attard family of Villa Attard, now represented in the person of Sur Benin, the last surviving member, had long been at crossed swords with the priest. Sur Benin's father had in his time entertained illusions of power over the small village, even after he had broken up his large estate and sold the pieces to the local farmers in order to pay off some of the considerable debts left over by Grandpapa Attard who seems to have been quite a wild one in his days, grabbing many a chance from among the foreign cabaret artistes of the time. When Dun Manwel had been entrusted with the parish, first the father, and now the son, had found cause for resentment: for here was a priest with a penchant for disrupting status quos, an active regard for his flock, and an irritating way of doing things which never seemed to require the slightest prior consultation with or authorization from the proud House of Attard.

"I hear that your project has fallen on evil times," Sur Benin said, smirking suitably. "Alas."

"Times will change, times will change," aphorized Dun Manwel, knowing his present weakness and the shrewdness of the other.

"I say Amen to that. Your faith is most commendable, Reverend. Pity it is not more infectious...But I cannot tarry. And why am I here, you might well ask?"

"Why are you here?"

"For one and one reason only."

"And that is?"

"To actually demean myself by offering you, well, yes, if you really must know, *help*—in the meantime hoping that my dear departed papa's deafness is still as chronic as it had always been."

Dun Manwel raised his eyebrows towards a chandelier upon which some flies had just begun dancing a pavane—of treachery, he mused!

"Indeed!" he pronounced—wisely, he hoped.

"Concerning the state of the church..."

"Yes? And what about the state of the church?"—very, very circumspectly.

"To put matters briefly...As the farm might, er, take a long time before it materializes, I personally feel it to be in the best interests of the people and—need I say it?—of that heavenly being with hands so within reach of those terrible instruments with which he could exact such dreadful punishments on whomever ignores him and his needs—you may have already gathered that I am referring to our illustrious patron saint, no less—if you, his *servant,* were no longer to postpone the setting in motion of the much needed repairs to the church—the said saint's domicile, need I be more explicit? With that holy end in view, I propose offering nothing more reprehensible than a considerable sum of money."

Dun Manwel groaned inside the shelter of his soutane. Ah, these Attard people! How cunning, how unscrupulous! If he accepted, he might as well, in the organist's slightly mystifying and, doubtlessly, *risque* mode of expression, kiss the farm good-bye, and, with it, the bright new church of the future. If he did not, well, what was going to hold his parishioners from voicing: "Truly he is no man of God. You mark my words, that Dun Manwel, that seductive handmaiden of the Devil will yet bring down the wrath of God upon our heads, and upon the heads of our children, and our children's children."

He turned to glance at the swollen grapes outside the window. Through the green tendrils, he saw the blue sky. The sky was the mouth; the grapes, the wisdom of true counsel. He returned his attention to his visitor.

"You must not think that I am not grateful for your offer," he began.

"God forbid!" said the other, thrusting a pious eye up the vaulted ceiling.

"But I'm less than disposed, let alone willing, to accept it."

Sur Benin leapt from the ancient chair which, in turn, sent strident, mindless echoes reverberating around the temple.

"So be it!" he uttered in the throes of a violent nervous tic. "Of course, I trust you do realize that you, and none but you, will have to bear the consequences of your ill-judged decision."

The consequences soon became apparent. News of Sur Benin's offer, and its rejection by Dun Manwel, spread rapidly through the village; and there, to see it keep its freshness, was Giomarija at his fanning and public relations best.

For Dun Manwel, matters went from bad to worse. The farm collection all but petered out. The people still turned up in church, but he could sense their deep wariness even while addressing them on such simple topics as births, marriages and deaths. "Just shut your big mouth, and get on with it," eyes, including the most somnolent, seemed to say. Worse still, doubts began to assail him.

Soon there would be no farm, and no new church; there, too, lurked the spiritual risk: let the people lose their trust in their pastor, and the Faith would suffer. He had betrayed the village and the flock entrusted into his care. Etcetera, etcetera...In the very act of crossing himself, his fingers took to prodding his forehead for signs of incipient horny bumps.

He pictured the turmoil on his account going on at the Archiepiscopal Curia in Valletta, with the Monsignors discussing him over their black coffee laced with extract of orange blossom—a concoction, incidentally, that was guaranteed to keep dyspepsia and other such galloping ailments at bay.

He should have been replaced long ago, he almost heard them tell one another in heavily contrived Latin. He has attained an age when one is not, er, completely in possession of one's, er, wits. In plain language, Dun Manwel is stark, raving...They would, in deference to charity, balk at the relevant word and instead intone "bonkers," deeming it a mild enough term for learned and saintly superiors to use—especially when its Latin synonym could be just about anything that was as unpronounceable as it was likely to be unprintable.

Dun Manwel would have borne all this, and more besides, with as light a heart as he could muster, had it not been for the most grievous blow of all.

It was not long before he began noticing that the members of the Committee were developing a predilection for whispering covertly to one another behind his back, averting their gaze whenever he chanced inside their line of vision, and, the moment he joined them, changing the subject and direction of their discourse to meteorological comments and prophecies—all stratagems invariably culminating in a series of hacking, debilitating coughs.

One day he knew he was alone. The schoolmaster had that morning come to tell him that he and his fellow-members would be nominating Giomarija to the Committee at the very next sitting...

At Giomarija's house, the schoolmaster had come straight to the point.

He had said: "You see, Giomarija, although we hold nothing against our *kappillan,* yet we are now convinced that this farm business is wrong. And, as we happen to know that your views coincide with ours, and considering the eminent stature you seem to have achieved in the village, would you do us the honor of joining us?"

"Join you? Where?" Giomarija had asked, eyes and moustache visibly gyrating and taking only a few seconds before his head took off to perform one dizzy spin after another.

"On the Committee, friend, where else?" the schoolmaster had reassured him. "Dun Manwel is too beaten to be able to object to your nomination. Besides we are five, and he is one. With you, we'll be six, just imagine! It would then be a simple matter, would it not, to cure Dun Manwel of his strange fixations, scrap the farm and commence with the church repairs forthwith."

Giomarija's eyes had glinted through the stratosphere. This was honor indeed! He had traveled far. At last he was truly a man of great consequence!

Besides, once on the Committee, would he not be in a better

position to further the interests of his friend and benefactor? He must ask Sur Benin for a new suit commensurate with his new status—and a new pair of creaky shoes to go with it. Socks, those abominable *suffocators* of good, honest, hard-working feet, must, he would have to insist, remain optional.

"I feel overwhelmed," he had said, hand on heart. And he had rushed to convey the news to Sur Benin, who chuckled, choked and said, "Good luck, Giomarija. It is the beginning of the end for the estimable padre. Who does he think he is—Mother Teresa? We'll soon take over, you mark my words."

Afterwards, it seemed to Giomarija the most natural thing in the world to have to listen to gentle hints dropped by the various members of the Committee to the effect that, being, as luck would have it, all family men with many hungry mouths to feed, they would be able to work his nomination better, and it certainly would give them better heart to fight Dun Manwel if, say, such a small thing as you-know-what crossed their palms...

"You see, Giomarija," remarked Sur Benin later, half-choking on his cigar and crème-de-menthe frappé, "they're all the same. Here, feed the rats, fill their maws." And he thrust a thick wad of notes into Giomarija's hand.

Giomarija did as his patron had directed. He fed the rats and, when they crept up for more, he did not once disappoint them. His zeal was so commendable that he even tried to slip in a few giant cigars as a kind of bonus, but none of the others seemed to have the stomach for them. However, not wanting to hurt Giomarija's feelings, they promptly suggested instead that they would be quite equally satisfied with the aggregate worth of the cigars, in cash, and—if they were not asking too much—at the retail price.

"Never was money better spent," said Sur Benin, thoroughly flushed with the heat of battle. "It could well be that this affair is costing me more than it is worth, but it is well and proper that I do it, for no man dare scoff at the Attards and get away with it."

Giomarija continued to shower largess upon the five members; and his back grew straighter; and his hat vied with the best right angle anywhere; and he grew a paunch which added those few extra kilos of authority to his person; and he fretted at the delay which was inevitable before he could reasonably aspire to the Chairmanship of the Civic Committee once Dun Manwel had retreated headlong in complete and utter confusion.

"Should have been put out to graze long ago," he mused, quite obviously metaphorically, on Dun Manwel. "Hee—hee."

His sermons at Lukrezja's took on a fresh line. He suggested to the good people that, as enough time had been wasted already, was it not most imperative to take the only democratic way left out of the impasse? Let the Committee decide once and for all! Let the Committee give the final verdict! And the citizens cried in unison, their voices washed along by free red wine: "It is as Giomarija says; let the Committee break the impasse! Let the Committee decide once and for all! Giomarija—who would have thought it possible?— knows what he is talking about, for is he not now a Committee member himself?"

Dun Manwel did not need much persuasion to call the all-important meeting. The die was cast! The dice were loaded heavily against him! He had lost! The sooner it was all over and done with the better it would be for everyone concerned. Besides, at least one lump out of the obligatory two had begun to knock for attention. The horniness, he thought aghast, fearfully averting his eyes from every reflecting surface that he passed, had begun...

On the appointed day, the Committee met behind closed doors after stationing four stalwarts of the village outside to keep the excited crowd back.

Dun Manwel, conscious of a newly forged weight almost above each eye, rose heavily to his feet. He looked with a doomed air at the members, now increased to six, and felt damning failure staring him in the eyes.

But he said to himself: "It is right that it should be so. I am one and they are six. How can six minds be wrong if the six all think alike? And all six are such good Christians. Ergo, am I one, too, or am I not?"

He heard the roll of thunder in the distance and felt it wise to begin at once.

"Gentlemen," he said, "I wish to commence my brief discourse by quoting an inspired and time-honored saw: *id est,* Man proposes and

God disposes..." He knew exactly whom *He* was going to dispose of...and where!

He said that he was prepared to shoulder all the responsibility and blame for the acrimoniousness which had enveloped his dear people of late. He had thought that with the farm he would truly be serving God and His people at one and the same time. How wrong he had been! He felt almost, but nay, he was *most* certain that it could not have been other than the Prince of Darkness who had planted the idea in his head in the first place. (Here he made a pretense of wiping his forehead.)

"My eyes have now been opened, and at the eleventh hour. *Mea culpa*...But let me not keep you from the crucial task. I should therefore request all those among you who feel that the money collected for the farm should instead be utilized in the interest of repairs to the church to be so kind as to raise their hands." He paused. "Heavenwards," he added, feeling he should make doubly sure his atonement and plea for forgiveness reached the right quarters.

He sat down wearily and closed his eyes.

Giomarija had throughout followed the preliminary proceedings with legs crossed, cigar in mouth, chewing his moment of triumph. Now, raising both hands as far as they could go, he turned around and with a broad smile scanned the falange of fellow-members.

The next instant he almost fell off his chair with shock and surprise, for his guerrillas were sitting quite placidly still with hands very much on their laps or held rigidly down their sides.

Meanwhile, Dun Manwel's face, now that he had reopened his eyes, was reflecting the depths of incomprehension.

"Come, come, gentlemen," he called, doubting whether they had heard him aright the first time. "Gentlemen, please, your votes for cancelling, er, kissing the farm good-bye." He felt that this time, all sense of propriety laid aside, he could not have been more explicit.

The schoolmaster was the first to rise from his chair and speak.

"Reverend," he began, "if you will permit me, I must raise a little matter before we cast our votes. Most of the perplexities that have afflicted us over the farm have all along been due to the problem of funds...Well, have they or have they not?"

"Indeed they have, my son," Dun Manwel concurred absently.

"Hear, hear," said the others in impeccable Committee fashion.

"If there had been sufficient money, the people would not have had time to grumble—not even for grumbling's sake, as they are so inclined to do—but, seeing the work begun, would have taken to it with enthusiasm and, no doubt, aplomb. That is, if there had been sufficient money...Before today, the money may not have been sufficient. Now, however, I, for one, find myself in an interesting condition; in other words, nothing now appears easier for me than to contribute a certain sum which will augment considerably what there is already."

And he went on to relate that a maternal aunt of his had died of a surfeit of fresh air right on top of Dingli Cliffs, but, happily, not before she had remembered him in her will. His inheritance from that source he would now pass on to the farm fund.

It was the organist's turn after the schoolmaster. He rose to announce that his paternal half-uncle had slipped to his death on the rocks of Long Island, U.S.A., leaving him a tidy sum of money, not much perhaps, but surely enough to cover the cost of at least half a dozen goats, including as many as three with kid, for the farm.

Then the other members spoke, each in his turn, relating woeful tales of grandmothers and long-lost cousins having the good sense to leave them extremely well provided for before they departed this vale of tears through over-eating or a too-negligent stance, as in one case, on the north-west parapet of the medieval citadel of Mdina. All this money, they were happy and privileged to aver, would now go to the farm.

Dun Manwel stared at them, speechless with wonder and surprise. "But, senators, wherefore hath thou withheld from me this goodly news?" he stammered in unwitting Latin.

The schoolmaster, reddening a little in the face, looked almost crossed-eyed at a spot above the priest's head when he said: "We, er, thought it would be, er, too unethical, your, er, Reverence..." and swiftly turned his full attention on Giomarija.

"And what about our friend and confrere, Giomarija?" he asked the brand-new member dulcetly. "Has he or has he not a little monetary contribution to make?" But, noticing Giomarija's face and fearing for his health, he raised the suggestion that, as Giomarija did not seem to have been as blessed as they in the matter of accommodating, and accident-prone, grandmamas and paternal half-uncles and maternal aunts and long-lost cousins, they should all agree to enter their collective contributions in the ledger as also including Giomarija's—though Giomarija's would, of course, forever remain an unknown quantity.

"And so," ended the schoolmaster, "the motion is defeated."

And, happening to observe Giomarija stooping to retrieve the remaining ten centimeters of his, as it eventually turned out, last cigar, which had had the nerve to fall from his fingers, he promptly added: "And by acclamation, too."

At which, he clapped; and all the others clapped, including Giomarija, after the schoolmaster had explained to him, with perhaps unnecessary terseness, what "by acclamation" meant; and the news, having been conveyed to the people outside, the people clapped, too.

"This is indeed the happiest moment of my life," sang Dun Manwel in the manner of one or another of the Psalms, while laying a kindly arm around Giomarija's shoulders. "My son," he went on, horny bumps now a thing of the past, "you are still the Giomarija of old, mourned times. And to think that I have doubted you! Tell me, will you not be my sacristan again?"

They say that, after Sur Benin Attard had gone to Giomarija's house that very same night and raised the question of vipers in the bosom, block-voting and the roof, he left the environs in a huff and went to live in a lonely hut in the fishing village of Zurrieq, where he plotted, with singular unsuccess, to organize the fishermen into planters of Sargasso pineapples.

As for Giomarija, he got his old job back and, from that point on, was much extolled for his punctual habits, and for his donkey's unerring timekeeping which, if the truth must be told, was all under the direction of the now pacified, and better seated, gods. And if sometimes the thought rankled in his head that the aggregate amount of the members' inheritance seemed to tally to the last half-cent with the amount he had distributed so liberally among them on Sur Benin's behalf, he never expressed it.

He continued in his old, old way, but, of course, with the new improvements, including his continued membership of the Committee where he was happiest when seconding motions, especially the more obtuse ones, which, it is on record, he did in the most impressive, and eye-catching, manner.

The Committee's minutes of proceedings go further to show (Vol. 3, p. 333, last line) that only once was a motion of his swiftly and decisively turned down by all present, and that was when he moved himself as a desirable candidate for the treasurership.

Born and raised in Malta, Francis Ebejer is a successful short story writer, novelist and playwright whose work appears in Malta, England and the USA. His early plays are credited with starting the modern theater in Malta. A bilingual writer (English and Maltese), he also writes and produces television plays. His short story "For Rozina...A Husband!" was published in SSI No. 20.

"We went to the pictures sometimes, and Annie paid so that it didn't affect my savings."

Just a Mild-Mannered Man

BY OLIVE WINCHESTER

I'M watching the sun's rays setting on my ambition—my store—and now it's wrecked. I'm waiting for the police, I didn't know what else to do. What can I tell them? I just don't understand. How did it all happen to me?

I always wanted to own a grocery store, or perhaps a delicatessen, just that much more of a specialist line.

I started my apprenticeship when I was fifteen, for a few shillings a week. My old manager taught me all the recognized swindles of the trade. He knew which boys stole, too, and would just stand at the door at night, holding out his hand for the spoils. And he never allowed the roundsman and the cashier to talk alone.

His wife used to come into the shop daily, and he would make out a bill for everything she took. Then, he'd pay the bill at the end of the week.

I knew from the start that I wanted to be a good grocer, like my boss, but I wanted to own a shop, not just be a manager. I dreamed of a short white coat, and a white apron beneath and a spotted bow tie.

Our cashier sat at a desk, all boxed in. She had endless columns of figures to balance before she was allowed home at night. This cashier was a funny girl. When other girls came into the shop and had a joke with me, she kept looking at us over the top of the ledgers. At first I thought she was just worried and cross, but one of the boys said, "She likes you Ernie."

The first place I took her was to the Derby. We rode over to Epsom on our bikes. Annie put a shilling each way on a horse—it didn't win. I couldn't spare money for betting because of saving every penny for my shop.

For the next three years Annie and I went out together...not really courting. I couldn't buy a ring. We'd walk through the woods every Sunday afternoon and eat high tea at her home and on Wednesday afternoons we'd walk on the common. I lived in lodgings, and the landlady wouldn't let me have anyone to tea unless I paid her. I couldn't afford that.

When the holidays came, I'd go home to Bognor to see my parents. Annie wanted to meet them. I thought it a bit soon for that.

When I got back we had an *understanding*. We went to the pictures sometimes, and Annie paid so that it didn't affect my savings.

Then the war came, and I was called up. I was placed in the Army Service Corps. (My feet were a bit flat, and I was shortsighted.) Never even got sent overseas, which was lucky as I didn't want to see foreign parts. After the war, my boss took me on again. Annie was still at the cash desk.

Annie came weeping to me one Sunday. I patted her and said, "What's up?" She started sobbing then, said her Mum wasn't going to feed me every Sunday forever. She shouted at me, "Proper mean you are, been courting me for eight years and never bought me a thing. If you don't marry me soon, I'm packing you in."

I was rather upset. I'd never looked at another girl. I thought Annie was happy with me. She knew I couldn't buy her presents and things.

So I said, "Well, we could get married in two years' time, as long as you keep working." My bank balance would grow well with both our monies. I'd take charge of her wages, as she was rather extravagant; she'd taken to using lipstick.

Annie was pleased about getting married and started to make plans. She'd grown tall since we first went out together and was much bigger than me now. Her mother let me in to tea again, as I was now almost one of the family.

I'll never forget the wedding. Annie looked well but it was a waste, really, that white dress. She didn't tell me before the day or I would have persuaded her not to buy it. There was such a spread too. I packed up what was left into bags, as we were going to my parents' home for our honeymoon.

Annie went in the sea—she had even bought a bathing suit. It quite spoilt the holiday for me. It cost money which could have been put to better use.

Annie stayed on at the cash desk, and my savings mounted up. Groceries were still rationed and often I'd sell some of our coupons—we didn't need to eat bacon or eggs.

We must have been married ten years when Annie got sick. She just collapsed at the cash desk. I was serving a good customer, so I couldn't attend to her right away. The boss rang for an ambulance and went along in it to the hospital with her, I took his place in the shop. It was an honor.

Luckily the next day was Sunday, so I could go and see her. She said, "The doctor says I'm to have a holiday." I thought she meant at her mother's. "No," she shouted, "I'm going to the seaside." "Don't be silly," I told her, "it'll cost too much." She started to cry, so I went home. She was too upset to see reason.

The next day I took in some flowers, and she cried and cried when she saw them. "They didn't cost anything, I just picked them through the fence from next door," I said. Then she got hysterical and threw her slippers at me, so I came away again. I was a bit angry with her for being so stupid.

I spoke to the doctor the next time I went to the hospital. He said Annie wanted and needed a baby. I told him we couldn't afford it yet. He was rude to me and said, "If people waited until they could afford children, few would be born."

The hospital sent Annie to a convalescent home and it was all free.

The boss was kind and paid her wages all the time.

She went back to the desk and the boss gave her a raise. I didn't know about it until she had had it a year. Then I found the envelope in her bag, and her raise had been given to her separately. She wouldn't give it to me, no matter how much I asked. I never felt the same towards her after that deceit.

The next year I bought my shop—a delicatessen with living quarters behind it. My ambition was realized by my own efforts.

Annie seemed to settle down after her illness and didn't mention children again. All my money had gone into the shop. Annie still refused to give me the money in the extra envelope. She helped in the shop but insisted on going away for a holiday each year with her friend.

I didn't like that friend. Twice a week she would come round. She and Annie would laugh together and sit drinking tea. They ate my biscuits too. They seemed to shut me out in my own home. So I would go and sit in the shop in the evenings, polish up the eggs and make everything perfect for the next day.

Annie wanted a cat—she said it would catch the mice in the storeroom—but a mouse trap was cheaper. Then she said a dog would be a good thing for burglars. But how could they get in with me in the shop in the evenings? She screamed at me then, "Why don't you sleep in your beloved shop?" It seemed a good idea to me, so I did, on a truckle bed.

For years our life continued in this way, quite happy and uneventful. I was saving for my old age now.

Trade dropped a bit when the supermarket opened. I didn't worry. I had my regulars. Then I heard two of my customers talking outside.

"What's the matter with Mrs. Race, going a bit queer isn't she?" one of them said.

"Yes, keeps giving short weight and laughing about it, doesn't she?"

I looked at Annie that night and said, "Are you all right?"

She laughed, "Would you care?" she answered.

I started noticing things. How she wouldn't come to serve people unless I called her, yet I knew she was peering through the curtains at the back of the shop. I had let her give change for a year or two, but now people often came to me and said they were short changed. I got cross. I'd worked for years for this store and I wasn't going to have her muck up my goodwill.

After the shop closed tonight I was going to talk to her.

She was in the living room feeding a stray dog with the end of a luncheon sausage. I was looking forward to that piece of sausage for my tea—and she was feeding it to a dog. I went to take it away from the dog and it bit me. I shouted at her and she shielded the dog as I picked up a chair to hit it.

"You miserable miser," she screamed at me, "all right, hit me, go on, I've eaten your food for years, hit me!" She was sobbing as she wrenched the door open and the dog ran out. Then she came after me, clawing at my face. I fended her off and she rushed screaming into the shop.

She threw pots of jam, eggs, all my precious stock, at the walls, on the floor. She hurled the scales and the weights through the windows. Then she ran out into the street—and she was laughing, laughing at me.

She's gone now. It's quiet. I can hear the siren in the distance. What can I tell them? I've never looked at another woman. What else could I have given her? I married her, that's what she wanted...wasn't it?

Olive Winchester is a grandmother with spirit. As a challenge, in 1979, she began studying at the University of Auckland for a B.A. After attending lectures all day, she enjoys disco dancing...and makes time for her own writing. Her story "My Rom" appeared in SSI No. 28.

"Nothing was asked, no tender word said,
no objection was uttered but a whimpered, 'Señor'..."

A Doll

BY MARTIJNE VAN LAAR

THE woman sat leaning against the peeling whitewashed wall of her dwelling. A large tatty sombrero protected her from the noon heat, her brown slender legs were stretched out in the sand and her hands rested in her lap like tired birds.

Nothing stirred except for the tail of a dozing mongrel vainly trying to chase the ever pestering flies, and a couple of hens in their never ending search for worms.

"Madre," a little girl followed by a cloud of dust came running towards the woman. Black pigtails dancing on thin shoulders. She was almost breathless with excitement. "Madre," she cried again, "I saw something, something so beautiful, beautiful...like an, an...you won't believe it..."

The mother shifted her sunshade a little away from her face. "What did you say? You saw something beautiful? Where? Here? There's nothing beautiful here." She shook the child. "Where have you been, Maria? Sneaked into the church again, did you? One day Don Pedro will catch you..."

"No Madre, it wasn't in the church."

"Where else would you...?"

"Oh, Mamma, I saw it, I really saw it with these," and pointing her grubby little fingers at radiant black eyes, she explained that she had seen a doll. "Like a little angel, Mamma, with a blue silk dress and golden curls."

"You saw what? A doll?" The mother uttered the last word almost in disgust.

"Yes, Madre, it was a doll, a real doll. Carmencita's father brought it for her from the town. Oh Mamma," and with a sigh as deep as an ocean, she turned her eyes beseechingly towards the silent heavens. "Oh, to have a doll like Carmencita's."

A child's dream returning to reality, a little toe scratching the sand. "Madre?" The child hesitated and the mother braced herself for the question. "Why haven't I got a father, who would bring me a doll?" No answer, no father, no doll. The child picked up a pebble and threw it at the clucking chickens.

Luisa was the second eldest of Jose's the coffee picker's thirteen children. A small undernourished child, aggressive in self-defense amongst her equals, but with a shy, inbred fear of her superiors. Her world, as for each and everyone of her class, was fenced in by the gates and boundaries of the great Estancia of Don Rodriguez.

Life centered around family and food; highlights were presented by the cycle of weddings, births and funerals. "They were all in God's hands," as Don Pedro told them regularly from his pulpit, and he knew and promised them, "Your reward in Heaven will be the greater the harder your sufferings on earth."

Beauty, marvel, happiness and riches seemed to be for the likes of Don Rodriguez and the Señora.

It was, however, at the time that Luisa was nearing her fourteenth birthday, that Lady Luck turned towards Jose the coffee picker. When the Señora sent word that Luisa was to present herself at the kitchens of the homestead to work as a scullery hand, there was great rejoicing amidst the family for this event meant one hungry mouth less to be fed.

Two years of working near the cooking pots had seen Luisa blossom into a lovely young girl with all the early seductive ripeness of her Latin race.

She was stringing beans when, on a hot sultry afternoon, Don Fernando, the master's eldest son strolled into the kitchen. The young man had just returned from the academy and was still dressed in his uniform.

With her hands behind her back and downcast eyes, Luisa made her obeisance, whispering, "Señor." The Señor took his time in selecting an orange from the huge copper bowl on the white marble table top and, at the same time, cast an approving glance at the girl.

After this, Don Fernando often came into the kitchen and each time Luisa felt her blood rushing to her cheeks under his glance.

It had been after another hot day when, in the short twilight of the tropical evening, Luisa walked back from her parents to the homestead. A thunderstorm was rapidly approaching and she started to run.

Suddenly Don Fernando rode beside her, reigned in his horse and with a big sweep of his strong arm lifted the frightened girl into his saddle and cantered off.

Nothing was asked, no tender word said, no objection was uttered but a whimpered, "Señor," when Luisa yielded to his passion. Neither veil nor orange blossom for Luisa, nothing but the smell of the fertile soil and the bitter-sweet fragrance of the flowering coffee trees.

They often met at dusk and sometimes she was ordered to his room. She kept calling him Señor. He never even asked her name. When his mood was playful, he would call her "My doll."

One night, with the smell of liquor heavy on his breath, he hung a rosary around her neck. "Pray for me, doll," he laughed drunkenly. "Pray for me, for I don't want to go to hell."

Then came the day when, driven by despair, she waited near the door of his room.

"Come over here, doll," he said and pointed to the place beside him. For the first time Luisa objected.

"Can't you see, Señor?" she pleaded softly. "Forgive me, please forgive me, Señor, for having to tell you, but..." The girl stretched her arms towards the man on the bed in an imploring gesture for help. Señor, Señor, please, help me, what am I to do?"

Enraged, the young man leaped from his bed and in a fury lashed out at "the slut, the whore, sleeping around with every farm hand on the Estancia." He ranted, "How dare you, you, you...trying to blackmail me into paying, me, your master." He grabbed a pillow and threw it at her.

She caught it and put her tear-stained face in the lace-covered down.

"Go!" he shouted. "Go, and don't you ever dare to show your face in this home again, or I'll kick you out personally."

Humiliated, drained of all feeling, even incapable of hatred, Luisa fled, clutching the pillow.

No, there was no room for marvels in Luisa's life. Even the birth of Maria was little more than a natural phenomenon, an added burden to the coffee picker's poverty.

The young mother never revealed the name of the child's father for what proof did she have? And what is a poor girl's proof if set against the might of the mighty? Luisa never questioned the ways of her God. But whatever joy and hope there had been in her young life had given way to bitter disillusionment, and the laugh on her lips had died with the prospect of a heavenly reward.

Maria's words, "Oh to have a doll like Carmencita's," had wakened the dormant anger in the mother's heart and at the same time touched a string of love. She felt a strong longing to give a little more to her child than a mere bellyful of beans, to give a little happiness.

The act of giving, however, is coupled to possessing and there was very little Luisa could call her own. That night she pulled an old cupboard box from under her iron bedstead and opened it. Apart from a simple white cotton shift, in which one day she was to be buried, it contained the lace-covered pillow as well as the one and only payment she had ever received for her sin—the rosary, "Pray for me, doll," that unusual glass-bead rosary which she had never dared to use. Instead of a cross it had a large purple heart. It was the only thing she could sell. But to whom?

For many nights the thoughts kept milling in her head and her courage built up; she would speak to Don Pedro, the parish priest.

One morning, after early mass Luisa knelt waiting on the cold stone floor until all worshippers had left. Her gaze fixed on the statue of the Holy Virgin, she listened to the approaching footsteps of the priest and softly she asked, "Father, may I speak to you?" However difficult it was to ask a favor of so holy a man, the mother managed to put her case before him. "...and would Father perhaps buy this rosary for the Virgin Mary and give her enough money for it so that she could buy that doll Maria wanted so very much."

The priest shook his head disapprovingly. "My daughter, what you are asking is an important thing. How could I do this, even if a poor priest like myself would be able to do it? If it became known, everybody would come with something to sell. No, my daughter, mine is a spiritual task. It's your soul that I'm concerned for."

The rosary lay in the palm of the woman's hand, a small heap of purple glass baubles. "And without a cross it is not even a proper rosary," the priest remarked. "Let me have a look." Holding and turning the rosary up to the light, Don Pedro seemed to change his mind. "Well...I'll see what I can do. I'll take it with me next time I go into town and maybe...with the help of our Blessed Mother..."

Then came the day when wading through the dust Don Pedro arrived, a box marked "Made in Japan" safely tucked under his arm. Maria got her doll. A doll with golden curls, dressed in blue silk, just like the Virgin Mary in the church, whose stoney hands were now adorned with an unusual rosary.

The light from the candles in front of her broke on beads and on a heart of flawless amythysts.

Born in The Netherlands, Martijne van Laar has been living in Cape Province most of her adult life. Many of her stories and essays reflect her extensive travels, some of the stories have been dramatized on radio. She has competed in and won several South African literary events.

"Christy, the barker and proprietor
of the enterprise, had suddenly got a problem,
though he didn't realize it instantly."

The Frog Lady

BY H.E. FRANCIS

AT four one Monday afternoon the yellow door of Jamiel's clothing
store, which had been empty and so much waste for many years,
was opened. Everybody who saw the big red letters SEE THE FROG
LADY—TEN CENTS stopped, and most of them got so curious
they had to see for themselves then and there. Nobody in town, after
all, had ever seen a frog lady, or even believed, in fact, that such a
thing existed. Outside, Donnie Matthewson himself hesitated. For
he had waited at the door, looking at the red sign, then at the dime in
his hand, dwelling on the risk of loss. He knew what a dime was, but
what was a frog lady? And a dime went fast if she was just a fake—he
knew that much.

So he stood outside with his idiot stare (everybody knows he has
scarcely an ounce of sense, because he was born without the
equipment)...he stood with that stare at the door and every time
someone came out he'd ask, "Is it a real frog? Is it?" But they got fog

in their faces and didn't answer or were filled with sadness or laughter which had a dirty sound—like snickers. You know the kind. And after a while he couldn't stand it any longer and handed his dime to the keeper, a man dressed queerly with colors men didn't usually wear like that: red and yellow and green all in a wide, striped ribbon shouldered and across his chest, then banded about his waist.

Inside, the arrow pointed immediately around the corner; and he could hear her singing the minute he got into the store. He stopped and the wild flutter of his eyes stopped too as if he saw something thrown up from deep inside him that was not really anywhere but just inside him. Whatever it was it made his face full of a look. He rarely had a look before. His face sags with a lapjaw, loose and uncontrolled, and his eyes droop into his cheeks—one of those faceless faces never explained, expressionless maybe because there's no learning held behind to mold it. I've heard his aunt say, "Poor Donnie's face wasn't even as good as the dead clay." At least you can take that in hand, lifeless as it is, and make a form and control it. And when you look at it, you can even get emotion from the sight of it, but what feeling can you get from Donnie himself?—though his aunt got some, because she'd cry sometimes. But that was long ago. She got over that. At least if she still cries, it must be inside.

Anyway he was inside the store, and he was stopped. It was the singing, it seemed. Or the song. You couldn't tell. But he went toward the sound with his head bent, a stealth in his steps as if he'd got a bird trapper or a thing in the bush the least shiver would scare off. He moved into the crowd around the voice. It was loud and nasal, growing in a big surge and falling, but always loud—

> *Let me call you sweethearrt...*
> *I'm in luuuuuuuuuuuvvv...*
> > > *wiiiiittttth...*
> > > > *youuuuuuuuuuu.*

She was sitting on an empty showcase, a huddle of flesh in a mound with her neck pushed into her shoulders; and her breasts hung into her belly indistinguishably. And it all sat on weighty thighs that seemed to stop at the knees where there were little knobs of toes on flat-bottomed fleshy pads that were her feet. But she stretched her head up into the air out of the flesh and sang—clear, loud, toneless—and her mouth wide like a fish after air...

> *Let me hear you whisperrrr*
> *That you luuuuuuuuvvv...*
> meeeeeeeeee...
> tooooooooo.

Tight around her, holding her bulk in, was a green satin cloth out of which her arms hung like her legs, only narrower, but with the same stubby knobs of flesh for fingers. He could not see her face, only her profile. When she ended her song everyone applauded, but he stood there and gaped. After, she took up a darning bag and pulled out blue yarn and needles and began to knit with two very busy hands. At that everyone applauded again. So she smiled and nodded thanks. She smiled all the time anyway, with lovely white teeth. Then she set the knitting aside and spoke:

"I am Erna. I am called the frog lady. I am twenty-seven years old and one of seven children; all the others are normal. I have ten toes and ten fingers (she directed the gazes to her feet, then held out her hands demonstratively). I move about without any help. I can cook and sew and I make my own clothes. I made this dress. We have been traveling for four years. Twenty-two states have seen me. I can sing and I read and write."

It came out fast and all without a breath between, like a speech learned. Finished, she held out a little tray the color of her dress; and without even knowing it, Donnie found himself looking straight into her face, with his hand on the tray. Still he didn't move; and catching the unexpected stillness, her gaze fell over him, held by his own. And her face blanked, disarmed, the smile went like a veil in the wind, leaving her face its nakedness only—like a reflection of the boy's face. But something else too...for the first time that night there was feeling: because she saw something, and it made sadness and warmth in her—

But the jolly crowd wanted more. The silence was not right for it, and a voice prodded her to sing again. Everyone laughed and egged her on: "Yes! Yes, sing!" Quickly she was caught up in their spirit and responded, laughed herself, but there was bleakness in her. Then she did her great feat—always made them applaud—took her needles, held them between her toes, and knitted. They loved it, gasped, sighed with awe and admiration, then pitied in relieved laughter. They forgot the boy. And at last she sang, still and smiling, the same song, in the same loud monotone among the giggles and people coming and going and the clinking of coins. And she sang loud with a wide smile and still eyes as the boy went out of the store back into the dying light of day and blinked, for he had seen the frog lady, and he didn't have a dime anymore, and he did not know what he had at all...

The sign said: ONE WEEK'S ENGAGEMENT.

"When is the week?" he asked the barker.

"Saturday night—that's the week. Five more days before we shove, Sonny."

The man looked at him, sizing him up, and chuckled to himself.

"Besides, we gotta get out for the big p'rade," he said. "There'll be nothin' doin' here for us with a convention in town. It'll be here, come Saturday. They'll be movin' too—men and animals all over the place."

"Animals?"

"Yeah," he said, "horses, lots-a horses." Donnie nodded. "And maybe others, the dog show," the man added. He nodded again, held by the man's talk. *Animals.*

"How old're ya boy?" the man asked, suddenly studying him shrewdly. A good-natured feel of his hand rubbed encouragingly on Donnie's shoulder.

A long time he looked at the man. But he said no more about the animals.

"Aw, come on, kid—what's the age? I ain't meanin' no harm. How *old're* ya?"

Agnes had told him to say it, but maybe it was the hardness in the man's asking or that he was still thinking of the frog lady he was going to see for the second time that prevented him. He wanted to go in bad now and he didn't want the man to stand with his bright stripes in the way.

"Ain't talkin', hey?" The barker was piqued. "I got no one to talk to all day," he said, " 'cept her, and she ain't good for much when it comes to talkin'. I as'ed ya becuz it was somethin' to say. Oh, what the hell!"

"My name is Donnie Matthewson," he said blunt, "and I live on Hope Street and my mother's name is Agnes Matthewson and I'm twenty-six." *There!*—now he'd said it by rote like Agnes always told him to say it if he was asked.

The man sullened a bit, looking hard at Donnie's smooth, unhaired skin; then he got back, getting the point, coming out of his denseness.

"Yeah," he said. "I guess ya mean it. Twenty-six. Well, whattaya know!"

Donnie could not understand what the man's look and tone said. Maybe he heard what was not right in the sounds, because there were some that set him all wrong and uncomfortable like hairs turned down the wrong way, and made twistings in his feelings so tight and uncomfortable; so he escaped, pushing past the man anxiously dropping his dime in the box, and went in.

—and there she was, sitting on the showcase as if she'd never left, encircled by a crowd thicker than last night's. He edged up close but someone cut in front of him, curious for a look at her limbs, and he ducked off and hung back farther with a silent waiting in him. From there he could hear her little speech just as well, and the *Let-me-call-you-sweetheart* number. That's when his head cocked, his eyes large on her, unmoving and unblinking...that tone shivering in him like the long sound of a new chord never heard before in all the world...

After the song the crowd thinned quite rapidly. Still he waited, walking around the room, coming nearer, then standing by the last man, listening to his questions. And as the man turned finally to head out the door, Donnie heard him talking to the barker, but not their words, because he saw her, and saw her smile fade, and her one automatic hold on the public gone. At his approach the tenderness came into her and maybe he felt some of the fluttering and throbbing in her as she looked at him. Because she held out her stubbed hands, and he could not resist it, the drawing of them. He went close and did not know what he was feeling. Taking his face between her hands, she looked long into it, over it, and touched it and pushed back his hair then to see all his face. But who could tell why? There was something between them, she knew that. Only she couldn't stand the restlessness of looking at his face anymore; she fidgeted at his hands, dropping her eyes...

When the barker came in a few minutes later he found her holding Donnie's hands, and there was a sound like quiet sobbing.

Christy, the barker and proprietor of the enterprise, had sudddenly got a problem, though he didn't realize it instantly. Only when Donnie came back the next two nights and sat with an unregistering face until he heard her sing, did Christy see the drawing come to life. *And wasn't Erna getting different, now he thought of it? Why the hell didn't he see it before? The kid had* sent *her maybe.* But when he told her that, she let him have a spiel about sick-and-tired of the racket.

"You're no fake, are ya? Then how the hell's it a racket?" he attacked her.

But she fretted. She looked out of their room into the bleak dark of the town she didn't know, except its name, Bristol, and she said in a longing, "It's like the town I come from, it's near the water and the air smells salty." She told him she could see the sand even. "You never seen wild roses, Christy?—pink, wild roses of the hot summer growing in the sand?"

What the hell did he know about pink roses, huh? He was a businessman. If he thought of pink roses, where the hell would they be?

Maybe he was thinking *Where are we anyhow?* because he scowled at himself questioningly.

But she answered him: "I would be back there."

"It's your own fault—*you* wanted this's well as I did. Was *my* idea, yeah, but you had nothin' to lose either. Ya only wanted to get out of that house where everyone was all right but you, that's all."

And it was true, she confessed it: *I went to him, I told him yes, I welcomed him like he was a church for shelter.*

"Yes," she said aloud, with a nod, weak and unable to fight

anymore.

In her simple way she knew she had gone down the glamour path in his mind, all because he had come in a whirlwind, high pressure and clear vision set in his words. It told her dreams could live. And she left the old lady who blamed both her and the old man for what Erna was—a freak. But they didn't know that a freak can think, she's got nothing else to do but think. She let Christy undress her down to this green satin piece and let the world see her for money.

He got a nice place in a town up-island, not far from Brooklyn, but in a few weeks he exhausted the possibilities. They set up in another town, then another, spending too much on fares, food and bed, not making enough. Drifting. They became irritable; then it would be right, calm...The feeling of skulking came over them as they began hiring dinky side-street stores, ex-shoeshine nooks, anywhere under the sun that he could perch her on a box and him stand outside where people went by. Sitting there, she saw her life, a headful of faces without meaning—only laughter sometimes; she could give them that at least—though sometimes hatred too; a headful of faces and dives, low joints—one-night stands, a week in a small town, a week in a big town sometimes, lucky...And the thick odors of people jamming close around her.

He left her in dirty rooms, calling her his sister who couldn't be separated from him—except when he went out, sometimes to get drunk and all the time to drink a little. Maybe the drinking explained the dirty rooms. Soon she was a burden to him, but he put up with her. At least he was smart, she was his bread-and-butter, she was useful anyhow. Everybody had to do something useful, didn't they? Well...?

In the dirty rooms she sat with her knitting, making sweaters and socks for Christy; and more and more she looked out the window, on the dark days especially, when the clouds thickened and the wind was a desolate blowing; and she forgot her knitting. Then it was that there was a big bleak dark space inside her, bigger than the day, too big for her, and she couldn't do anything about it. She sat, and looked into the vast sky, and she forgot her knitting...

But on the fourth day in Bristol she stopped knitting in her spare time.

"What the hell'd you quit for?" Christy asked when she told him she'd put it away for a while. Maybe so she could go on sitting in a slummy room on Thames Street, looking into the harbor...And sea gulls flew white into the gray November sky. A smell of sea came in, lingering, and grease from the restaurant downstairs. But she didn't say all that.

"I don't know," she said. "I can't, I don't want to."

"OK! Forget it," he said. He let it go at that, because her glance was heavier than before, though all the time he was thinking about how it shouldn't make any difference anyhow if she wanted to knit or not off the job. Only he couldn't hold back, asking testily:

"Only you'll knit on the job?"

"Yes, on the job," she said, comprehending, but already she was caught in the graceful swoop of gulls outside and that was the end of their talk, until the fifth morning...

...because something happened.

It was happening last night all the time he was out front yelling SEE THE FROG LADY. ONLY TEN CENTS, ONE THIN DIME in the only language he knew, over and over. He couldn't see it even when he was standing inside, watching the bastard little idiot again and watching Erna, because he didn't know where it was going on. But even she and the idiot boy didn't know that. Maybe it was because Christy couldn't see it that he yelled louder and walked up and down faster and glanced back and forth into the store and then walked some more. He smoked fast, twice as many cigarettes, and stomped and ground on them, heavy. For something was in the whole room and he did not understand what.

It was worst of all when she sang, because it was the same monotone but the voice was different or the measure or...what was? Word about the frog lady had spread fast. There were more people tonight than ever. He should be happy as hell about business being so good. But he wasn't; he couldn't get through this feeling. It had nothing to do with the crowd in the room or the thick tobacco smoke he couldn't see through. But he felt a thickness there that filled the room and made no room for him in it...and he did not know, that was the thing. ...O, what the hell!

SEE THE...FROG...LADYYYY, he yelled, *TEN*-CENTS, calling it loudly down the long main street, knowing it was barren at this hour.

From the door he watched her shadow cast on the wall, its shapeless mass, its arms raised above the heads. He saw her through part of her last performance, then went back out to smoke in the cool air. The customers came out noisy and went down the sidewalk into the streetlights. Now he had to tell her it was time to leave, she could pack up.

"You go now, huh?" he said to Donnie, who looked blankly until Erna nodded yes, making him actually smile. Then he went out the door.

"How come ya not waitin' for me?"

While Erna put her knitting and her change-plate in the carrier, put a tam on and threw a heavy coat about her, Christy paced impatiently. He offered to help her down but she had already slid to the floor and seized the bag herself. She didn't even ask him how much money they made tonight. And her walk was settled and firm.

"Erna...?"

She halted, thrusting her head boldly back, with no effort to turn herself. She was inquiring coldly. Not like Erna. *Well? What is it? I'm waiting...*She waited while he blew smoke, then turned indifferently away.

"Where are you going?" he said in a voice of almost-not-being-able-to-take-any-more.

"To the room," she said, "where else?"

"How come ya not waitin' for me?"

"..."

"What're ya doin?" He plagued at her, begrudging the silence. "What're ya thinkin' a doin? Whatta ya think I am—nobody? I'm Christy. *Christy,* ya hear?" But her silence made him feel pushed aside.

"What'd *I* do?" he said. "Ya mad—well, what'd *I* do?" He paced up and down, flung his hands out at her, asking her *what'd he do?*

"It's that kid!—that God-damn blitherin' idiot comin' here three nights straight!"

"He's not an idiot, he talks sense when he wants, he talks to me fine." What was the difference in her voice? Filled. What was empty didn't sound empty anymore, but even soft and it surprised him so he couldn't say without stuttering or something.

"Erna—"

He saw her stiffen with protection or anger or indifference perhaps—he'd never know—but she got herself away, and he swore as she went to the door.

"Wait," he called after, "I'll take ya home."

He pulled out his watch, scanned it anxiously, telling her it was too late for her to be in the dark by herself, she might fall, they might not open tomorrow night, he'd better see her safe. He put the watch back in his pocket, thinking *why didn't he let the kid stay, all because of the kid! Damn!*

"No," she said.

"What's the matter with you?" Now his bungling made confusion and rage in him. "I'll take ya home."

"No," she said. She pushed the door out and the cold night came in. "I am not a gold watch," she said disdainfully and padded heavily out into the street. And the door came closed between them.

And that's what happened; but for a minute before he left the store he stood there realizing that it had happened, and he still did not know what it was...

In the morning she went out early—rare for her who usually slept late—and did not show up until lunch, and then only briefly. Never before had she left without telling him where she was going.

But Christy knew small towns and the corner gab. He knew the simple trick: you talk around until you get to the immediate point, which at first you made seem the remote point. So everything is an accident; and nobody is blamed for telling...

—the two were seen walking across the Common under trees bare in the dead cold, their voices crystal clinks and their steps scrapes on the echoing ground. They didn't mind the cold, walking close, talking: nobody ever heard Donnie talk *that* much before. At the waterfront they stood on rocks, hearing waves and the windbeat, and watching the seaspray and holding hands. They came back into town along Hope Street with indifference toward everyone. And this time she walked him home.

That is what the town told Christy. What he couldn't know without her telling it was their other two meetings while Christy was drinking, or how they'd agreed to meet, right in front of Christy himself, when Erna had nodded yes to Donnie last night. Or he couldn't know about Donnie's mother waiting for Erna; or of the woman's own warped love. For Mrs. Matthewson knew about the meetings. In a clarity baffling even to her—coming from his head as it was—Donnie had told her.

"She is a frog lady," he had said.

Erna held out her hand that was not even like a hand and said, "Hello," clearly and forward without shame. That pleased Mrs. Matthewson, who had been made an outcast from the town by its pity, the thing she hated and grieved over as their most merciless sin against her. But Erna came, not knowing this, so it gave the woman a rare warmth for the girl.

At last Mrs. Matthewson told Erna what she had hoped.

"I've watched him all week," she said. "He tells me what he can, you know. After the first time, I wanted very much to meet you, Erna. Did you know I went downtown and stood in the crowd to see you because the first day he talked so of you?" She did not tell of the first hurt of seeing Erna, because it was a small thing to the pleasure the girl brought to Donnie and her, his mother, at seeing it in him. Not only that, but she feared Erna's leaving town, because she never could know Donnie's mind or what it would make him do. But they must talk it out. Rather, she talked it out.

"It is scarcely a rash judgment, Erna. Fast, yes, but we have short lives, we must grasp the right things when they are here. I've a good bit of money and I'll do anything to make Don happy. And you, Erna—can you live this life of wandering to maintain yourself for long? If something should happen to you or to your partner...but, of course, that is too unpleasant to think of.

"I have this big house and I'm a lonely woman..."

And Erna could not say...Her hands. Floundering.

"He is my whole life, Erna," the woman said. Above all things, she loved him, glancing at her whole fragment, "And he is so fond of you already. He's never really been fond of a person before, you know.

Oh, you could make us very happy and we would both try very hard to do the same for you. I think we would succeed, Erna."

And in the tremendous awe of it, Erna did not know what to do, only say *Yes! Yes!* it was all so wonderful that it hurt. Yet she did not comprehend everything until she was outside and the meaning came clearly: it meant change, and no Christy, and the goodness of the woman, and the house, the lovely house, and she could help someone at last—Oh, that above all she wanted and so desperately that she could not do without it now—ever. But how could that come suddenly in five days? How could life change so? How? But there was only the quiet of the late afternoon darkness...

By the time she returned to Christy she was talkative, with a nervous animation, and a plan she feared—the first she'd ever had—but she did not get to tell it to him—not yet. For she had to sit through his rantings—*her showing herself to the whole town free! How the hell could they make any money? Who'd come to see her now—and what were they supposed to do, starve? She trying to get down with a cold or something? Did she know what she was doing? What got into her anyway? And them leaving in two days and never coming back anyhow—*

Then she spoke out:

—but she could never come back, she said, she was not leaving, you see...

"Whatta ya mean!"

So she told him what happened in that house this afternoon.

"O, please, don't be so mad, Christy," she pleaded. "They're only meaning to be kind."

"And that's what kindness is—huh? Does a man out of a job!"

"Please, Christy!"

" 'Please, Christy! Please Christy!' That all ya got to say after all I did for ya? Is it? Well *is* it?"

"For me...?"

"Yes—*you!* An' you used-ta say we got everythin' we need—what more we want *You*—not me!"

"But we haven't any more, it's not the same now, I got more."

"What? *What?* I ask ya. Tell me what ya got now you didn't have before. A house? Ya want a house, is *that* it?"

"..."

"Well?"

"I don't know."

"There! What'd I tell ya? You're not in love with that—"

"Love...? Her face questioned curiously as with discovery.

"—idiot!"

"Love..."

"Now what's the matter?"

"That's what I have," she said. "I didn't have that before, Christy. Never..." They had said the word she could never say, the word she could only sing but never say.

"Have what?"

"Love," she said, rolling it softly. Because at last they had said it, what was hid, and she knew.

Filled with the sound of her own self thinking it, she scarcely heard him, and her quiet infuriated him so that he broke into shouting she couldn't do that to him.

"Ya got responsibility, ya don't let people go like that. We got somethin' together—yes, *us!*"

He was close with a mad look she had never seen in him. She held up her stumped hands..."Christy!" It bunched out, she couldn't find words, only that one over and over. But he only stood by her. She rolled then, deep-breathing on the bed, as he turned to the window, not knowing anymore what to say. And their hard breathing made a heavier silence that held them as if they couldn't move anymore.

Worn out, yes. But what could she do? It was time to have a bite, to go back to the store together, for him to yell and her to sing: and the evening would come down slow and long and heavy between them.

All through the evening, she knew he was watching. He barked less and if she looked she could see his shadow on the front panes, walking. She went on singing and talking and watching the shadow. But after, it was Donnie who walked her to her door and told her not to forget tomorrow at his house.

In the room she couldn't get the house out of her mind; she sat with all her clothes on in the bed, rolled over—the warm cozy house, the woman like a mother, and Donnie...In the darkness his face came to her and she heard how Christy always said the word *Donnie,* to make her sick inside because it brought the boy's face back and her feeling as she saw it on Monday in the crowd; that she would like long fingers to reach out with and stroke that face into movement—because it looked like a plate, empty, and it stared; because it did nothing, like her own body, and herself, nothing. Ah...she knew that so well, so she would like long hands to touch him with and to make him feel. For he had done that to her, deeply. Now Mrs. Matthewson would make it possible for her to do something, for she had never really done anything for anybody before...

When Christy came in—ranting again—she was already so filled with thought she could not listen to the words. She lay unresponsive and felt no connection with anything. She was Erna alone now, the first time she knew who she was, and she thought, trembling, the first time she was a woman and could make a decision...

Sometime deep in the morning dark she woke from a doze and rolled her head round toward the window, the barely visible frame. And there was the red cigarette and Christy's face faint when he puffed a glow. At her movement, the glow rose and she heard his steps back and forth in the room, and she could discern the black, moving Christy, a shadow too...She tried to doze again, but it was a long night, and thoughtful; and she figured how Christy was a shadow on her, how all people are shadows on each other...

In the morning she found him in the chair asleep, still dressed. When she put a blanket over him, he twitched, looking at her with eyes red from lack of sleep and staying out half the night and not sleeping the night before. They were tired and not Christy's, she thought, but they were not different either. How could that be? It had not occurred to her before, but she had never seen them true, never looked really. But he had her hand and said: "You can't go. You gotta stay. We're no good alone, 'specially me," and he dropped her hand.

"That's not so—" she said, not sure now, never sure now with the night gone. "I can be something to them. I'll make them happy. I can do it, Christy, she said so. *I* can make them happy." Her voice rose, frenzied. She wanted to beat him and make him know she could make them happy. She wanted to beat it into him until he said *Yes!*

Go...go! and admitted she could do it and gave her a reason for going. But his head rolled drunk-tired. Her hands fell, nothing came out of her, but his words were unexpectedly sore in her, burnings..."Erna. ...I need you, Erna."

Why did he have to say *that* again?

She panted down the stairs, holding tight to the bannister, and went into the cafe.

"Cold, 'ey?" the Italian said. Because she didn't reply with her usual cheer that he liked so well, he went behind the counter and waited. The entire meal was like that—him waiting and Erna sitting and eating quietly. Finally she left silently, leaving him puzzled.

Outside, the chill was good, made Erna alive in it as perhaps she'd never been before. Mrs. Matthewson expected her early. As she walked she grew happy with the strength of her decision. She could not yet believe a week could make a life so different. There was early morning noise in the town, quickening because the holiday was coming. It all made her laugh audibly. But near the house the joy went, she became upset and strange, and when she saw Mrs. Matthewson she did not have the conviction that had come over her partly in bed, then wholly at breakfast, so she sat in a tremble and maybe from fear or shame began right away speaking, jerky.

"Why, Erna dear, what is it? You must be more plain than that," Mrs. Matthewson said. "Whatever are you trying to tell me?"

"I don't know what it is," she said. "I thought if someone liked you it was easy. You could like back and that was all and you could go anywhere or do anything. Like Donnie—because I made him happy and it made me happy to do it, see—? And I thought: that's all there is to it. But it's not. It's just he woke me up and I never was awake before—see? It made me be so strong. I never was before, I mean. Oh, I *want* to stay—more than anything—with you and him, but that's wrong 'cause what would I do then, huh? Well, that's what I *thought* would be so nice and it *would*...but then it would hurt too, because I got what *I* want—and where's Christy then?"

"Erna..." The forlorn world inside the woman returned. She saw the foreboding *no* in the girl, gently given, but still *no*. And she knew the old truth—out the window was the town and it could be no different out in the world—that it was only the girl's excitement after all and her own, that they must grow slowly and they had had their life with one another quickly in a few days, and that was no whole growing.

"You have changed your mind, yet it would have been so good for all of us. But you must think what might happen—"

"That is what I thought. Only Donnie's got you to look after him and I'd have you too. See?—I thought I'd help—and I would—but you don't need it bad as Christy does now. And it's something else too too: life—it's not being easy-living and warm and with always the sure thing behind you—"

She was close to the woman, she talked excitedly and fierce power came in her: that she could be the cause of this. Donnie. Or Christy. Both of them in need. And one would be unhappy—and she the cause. For a moment there was a strangeness in this new thought: *it is me who was nobody, nothing to nobody*—me, *Erna*.

But Mrs. Matthewson could not know what she was thinking. She had her arm about the girl, smiling.

"How you have *seen* things, child," she said, rising, going to the window. "We'll be very sorry. We'll miss you."

Missed. But she could not stand it all at once—all the joy or what it meant, love, the power, the discovery too big for her.

"So you are certain you will not change your mind?" It was her last attempt, hopeless, she knew. "*Are* you certain, Erna?"

She could say *no*. But there was Christy lying in the chair, Christy's red eyes and desolate voice, and their long, weary, sweating drag into everywhere and together, that had not ended. Oh, she was wise: it would never be love that she could have, but she had a right, hadn't she, to a kind anyway. What he said...need.

Rising, she felt tall and caught at her fingers, feeling for a minute they were long like the ones she wanted to soothe Donnie's empty face looking at her. But of course they weren't. No matter. They didn't matter at all now.

She felt the towering in her. "I cannot tell you," she began. And she could not, because she didn't know the word for all that: giving up the woman and the boy, yet towering in the joy of it...She tried to understand. "When you give up something you want, you're supposed to be sad..."

Yet she smiled, waving to them both—to Donnie behind, a kiss. She knew the woman understood, as she went out into the crisp, clear air...And there was a happiness in her because she could look back—perhaps no one would ever miss her again, but already she could say: *somewhere I am missed, I made someone care, they want me to come back.*

She trudged down the street, glad because she would be with Christy, she had made him need at last. Somehow it was very right, that was a kind of love; and they both knew it, she felt...

That evening after closing, while the Saturday night bonfire in celebration of the coming holiday blazed in the sky, she and Christy stood waiting at the railway station, two black figures against the orange glow the other side of town. Erna laughed into the flaming sky, thinking how she was with Christy because he needed her and he might change at last; and how Donnie would be sitting in that house, lonesome for her...Beside her, Christy sighed deeply with relief, setting down the bags, thinking how clever he was he'd got her to stay, maybe he'd stash a little cash away for later on, but just now they had lots of time, why not a drink before train time...?

And close to the bonfire Donnie roared with a nondescript gurgling laughter as he warmed his side joyfully and watched the mascot goat brought for the Monday morning parade. It wore a colorful American Legion patch on its back, and Donnie reached out his long hands to pet the goat with all the tenderness of new-found love.

H.E. Francis, a busy literary person, has several short story collections to his credit. His stories also appear in anthologies and magazines, along with his skilled translations of works by Spanish and South American writers. His translations have appeared in previous SSI issues. In addition, he teaches at the university level and is the founding editor of Poem *and poetry editor of* This Issue.

"We were both lucky we didn't freeze to death,
falling asleep like that."

Uncle's Bargain

BY YALE SUSSMAN

OF course, back then (I'm talking now—what?—around the first of
December, nineteen fifty-four?)—back then it was almost a crime for
a Jew to be dealing in Christmas trees. Even now I wouldn't bother
selling them except that I have to—I didn't tell you this story before,
did I?"

So far, it had been one of the few stories Uncle Seymour hadn't
told and retold every time I visited him. He and Aunt Nora had no
children and I was, if I may say so, his favorite nephew. As such, I had
always considered the lending of my ears as a form of "dues" to be
paid to my uncle. But this story was new to me. I knew he sold
Christmas trees every year, but I never thought about it much.
Perhaps this was a trick: would Uncle's Christmas trees eventually
weave themselves into one of his old familiars? Maybe the one about
his grocery being vandalized by the family beagle? Suspicious of a
switch, I tried to get comfortable in the padded kitchen chair, folded

my hands together on the table and answered, warily, "No, I don't think so."

Uncle Seymour smiled as he lit a cigar.

"Good. I want you to pay attention, so you'll know why I invited you here today. Like I was saying, years ago people thought it was even more *meshugeh* (crazy) than now. Everybody, Christians, Jews, everybody. My father, may he rest in peace, was against it. He said, 'Seymour, only a fool *schlepps* (trudges) way up to Canada this time of year. For what are you going? Christmas trees? You'll get caught in a blizzard with Lester's old truck, you'll freeze to death and get eaten by an Eskimo.' Those were his very words.

"Of course," Uncle Seymour went on with a slow nod of his head, "my Poppa wasn't the only one. The entire *shul* (congregation) really made a fuss about it, especially the Felds, Herman Feld and Izzy Feld and their brother-in-law, Maurice Bernstein. They said it wouldn't look right. They were always sticking their noses in where they didn't belong. I remember even my mother saying that the Felds and Bernstein were the three biggest *yentas* (gossipy old women) in the Catskills. But still, I thought at the time, maybe they were right. I must have been only a little older than you, what did I know? Sure, ketchup I knew to take from a case and put on the shelves, six-packs of soda I knew, quart bottles I knew. Cartons of milk, cigarettes. But what in hell did Sy Kaufman know about Christmas trees? I told that to Lester Burlingame when he asked me to be his partner, his 'money man.' But he said he wanted me anyway. So I went.

"Lester was a real old-time farmer. I knew him from when he sold eggs to my father's store. His family had been living on the same farm for years and years, probably ever since Rip Van Winkle. Lester did some hauling with his truck, he did odd jobs, he raised chickens, some cattle, and the year before what I'm talking about, he went up to Canada to bring back a load of Christmas trees. That year he had the Crounse brothers for his partners. They were supposed to put up the money to buy the trees, Lester would do the buying and hauling back from Canada, and they would all take turns selling them from a corner lot. They were supposed to split the profits fifty-fifty. Well, the Crounse brothers were crooks, which everyone but Lester knew. And then Lester found out, the hard way. So the next year he asks me to be his partner. I hear about how much money we can make, and back at that time, when I was still young, I had a dream to eventually expand the grocery into a chain of fancy supermarkets. And then I could make money and afford to be a big-shot too, and get awards and thank yous for all my donations to the charities."

Uncle Seymour paused for a moment, tapping his cigar thoughtfully. "Fame and fortune," he said. "You can see what happened on both accounts.

"Anyway, there we are driving around the wilds of Canada in Lester's old flatbed truck. There isn't much snow on the ground, but it's cold as hell and he's taking us past Quebec City into Godforsaken backwoods where no one lives except this farmer, Gilbert, that sold the trees to Lester the year before. Well, the two of them start out friendly enough, but they wind up in a big argument, a real shouting match. Lester wants to pick and cut his own trees like he did last year, and Gilbert says he has to take what's cut already or pay extra. It's eighty cents to take the ones already cut, a dollar twenty-five to cut our own. So Lester examines the piles of cut trees behind the barn and he tells Gilbert we want to cut our own trees, but at the old price, eighty cents. And they go on and on about it. Finally, Lester tells Gilbert to keep his lousy trees and we leave.

" 'Them trees was only wall trees,' Lester tells me back in the truck.

" 'Wool trees?' I ask him, and he says, 'No, wall trees, the kind where the needles fall off on one side and they're only good for putting up against a wall. Sure, they look akay now, but give them a week and you'll see how brown they get.' Lester figures that Gilbert probably had cut the trees for someone else who was going to put them into cold storage, then that deal fell through so Gilbert wanted to stick us with them. 'Well,' Lester says, 'let him stick them back in the ground, after all the business I gave him last year.'

"Which is fine for him to say, but now that we've *schlepped* all the way to Canada, we've got no idea where to go next. Gilbert was the only guy he knew. And if you don't have a good contact for the trees you really pay through the nose for them. So it doesn't look good for us.

"The first town we hit, Lester says he's thirsty and we find a tavern. Pretty soon it's late, so we find a guest house for the night, but then he goes back to the tavern while I try to get some sleep. I remember thinking in my bed there, what the hell, even if we don't get any trees, at least I finally got to see Canada. And I fall asleep.

"Suddenly, in the middle of my sleep something violent happens to me, I'm being physically shaken out of my dreams. My first thoughts are about the cash I'm carrying, seven hundred dollars in my pants pocket. But I'm not used to the room, where are my pants? Then there's a little crash as someone stumbles against the bedside table, then the lamp turns on and it's Lester. He plops down on the side of my bed like a ton of bricks, smelling from alcohol and tobacco, and he says, 'Wake up, you old peach fuzz, wake up. You won't believe it.'

" 'Lester,' I yell at him, 'I thought you were a burglar! Don't ever scare me like that again! Are you drunk? Are you all right?'

"So Lester tells me he's fine and that he passed being drunk hours ago (it's now about three in the morning). Then he starts yelling over and over that he got us trees, he got us trees.

"It seems when Lester was at the bar he got to talking with some local people and one of them was an Indian. Lester gets talking about trees and the Indian tells him there's an Indian reservation about seventy miles north of the town and they've got a whole forest of young trees they'll practically *give* us and we can choose and cut our own. And best of all, the Indian says they'll dicker, so who knows how cheap we might get them for? Both Lester and I see dollar signs in front of our eyes. I tell Lester it sounds too good to be true, and he admits there is one possible hitch. It seems the road to the reservation isn't too reliable, seems it's one of those mountain dirt roads that's barely wide enough for one car. A lot of people wouldn't go on it this time of year, but it's okay now, the Indian says it's driveable. The thing is, if it does snow bad, then the only way we can get out is with a team of horses. But the Indian tells Lester it isn't supposed to snow for a while yet, and Lester says anyone will tell you that Indians know all about nature and the weather. Lester's convinced, he says it's the best deal he's ever heard of for trees and he wished he'd known about the Indians the year before. He says the Indian from the bar will even go with us to show us the way. Then

Lester leans his face in even closer to me on the edge of the bed, and I can see how his face is puffy from all the alcohol and not getting any sleep and how bleary-eyed he is. 'Sy.' he tells me, 'tomorrow I want you to do all the bargaining with the Indians.'

"I'm in shock! I tell Lester I don't know anything about Christmas trees, that I never bought even one Christmas tree before in my life, but he just smiles and says it doesn't make any difference. He says he never bought Christmas trees from these Indians before, either. Lester tells me that he messed up with Gilbert earlier, that there should have been some way he could have bargained with him. So he wants me to do the bargaining with the Indians because, he says, he just has a feeling that I should do it. Then Lester stands up and falls into his own bed. He tells me to wake him up in two hours so we can pick up the Indian out on the farm where he's the hired hand. Want some tea?" Uncle Seymour asked me, suddenly rising from the table to light the gas under the kettle.

"Sure," I said. "So did you get the trees cheap?"

"Don't make me get ahead of myself," he said, sitting down again.

"The Indian's name was Arthur Goodrich, so go and figure names. He was about nineteen or twenty, a good kid, quiet. Well, in some places the road Arthur showed us was not much bigger than a deer path and just as winding, I'm not exaggerating. It slowly went uphill into mountains and for the last thirty or so miles it wasn't even paved. From the road we can see lots of deer and a beaver dam and even a bear in one place. But, like Arthur Goodrich promised, there wasn't any snow to speak of, so the truck was okay.

"Arthur wasn't very talkative, he just hummed a lot. Lester did most of the talking, telling dirty jokes and swearing at the road. And believe it or not, I didn't have much to say so I just shut up. I was young then.

"I had never been on an Indian reservation before, so I didn't know what to expect. I didn't really expect wigwams, but I wasn't ready for what I saw. All of the houses were huddled together in one area, if you could call them houses. The best of them were only shacks with that cheap shingleboard covering, and all of them were in exactly the same color and pattern, like they had all gotten it wholesale someplace. But most of the shacks only had tarpaper on them and don't forget, this is winter. Also, a lot of them lived in old beat-up house trailers, the real small kind. One family was even living in two yellow school buses welded together. You could tell nobody made out too good there. Some kids were playing outside and almost every one of them had torn clothes and rotten teeth. It was sad. It seems they had this one section of land for their homes and all the farmland nearby was common land that they all worked together. That's where they kept their skinny cows and sheep, too.

"Well, Arthur Goodrich leads us to one of the sturdier shacks and introduces us to the Chief. Now guess what his name was."

"Sitting Bull."

"No. Guess! You won't guess in a million years."

"I don't know, Unk."

"Just guess."

"I don't know—Mendal Leibowitz, right?"

Uncle Seymour closed his eyes and smiled at me.

"Not bad. Close. Would you believe Sidney Bearman?"

"Sidney Bearman," I repeated, shaking my head. "Only you could find an Indian named Sidney Bearman."

"Let me go on. Not only is his name Sidney Bearman, but he looks exactly, I mean exactly, like my Uncle Hymie who you never saw, may he rest in peace. Same tiny bird's beak, same sad eyes, same big ears. Of course, he didn't talk like my Uncle Hymie. He spoke pretty good English, not Yiddish. Still, it was a shock, like seeing something out of the long ago past. Anyway, Arthur Goodrich explains what we want, so Sidney Bearman grabs a coat and takes us with some of his men to the forest nearby. All around there's really nice young trees, just what we want. Lester pulls me aside and says that usually in a load of trees you get some that sell for six bucks, some seven and some eight, but all of these will go for seven and eight. And no wall trees. Lester still wants me to do the bargaining and he's sure we can get the trees real cheap on account of the Indians need the money and will take whatever we offer them.

"So there I am, out in the middle of an open forest, trying to find out how much Sidney Bearman wants for a load of Christmas trees, and all the while I have to keep back a smile because it's like I'm dealing with my own Uncle Hymie, may he rest in peace. Finally,

Sidney asks for thirty-five dollars for a whole truckload of trees. I'm speechless. Who would think that's all they would ask for? There's just no sense haggling with that low a price, it wouldn't be proper. And Sidney says his men will even cut down the ones we choose and load them on the truck.

"Well, we get about seven hundred trees, we tie back the branches, then we tie them together in twos and threes, and it's late when we finish loading, it's dark and it's cold. We go to Sidney's house to settle up and we salute the deal with some homemade moonshine they pass around. It tastes like blackberries mixed with ground-up pine cones. Not exactly Manishewitz, but it grows on you—Lester even bought a jug to bring back with us. And we're having a fine time, especially Lester, we're all kibbitzing and it's almost like we're all old buddies. I'm almost ashamed when I pull out my thick wallet and take out a measly thirty-five dollars for these pitiful people. It's funny, with all that cash showing in front of those strangers I don't feel the least bit worried, and I know they could use the money.

"We go to leave, but Arthur Goodrich wants to stay behind on the reservation for a few days and Lester says it's okay, he knows the way back. So we climb back into the truck and wave good-bye, and right away Lester and me see the dollar signs again, and I'm thinking about my chain of fancy supermarkets. Well, we haven't even gone ten miles when without warning the snow begins to come down thick, I mean like a blanket. I can still see the big square flakes that plopped down on the front windshields. Lester is driving very slow now, in low gear. I ask him if he's all right, on account of the moonshine, and he says sure, he could drive back blindfolded. We go another five miles and you can't hardly see on account of the snow. Lester has to be real careful going downhill with the full load, and he has to curse his old truck to make it go up the hills. A deer path. That's all he has to drive on, and now it's getting covered over so you can't see the road, only the trees and boulders on either side of it. We take turns getting out to clean the windows, but still we can't see and we're both holding our breath. You could hear a pin drop, except for the motor and the defroster fans.

"Then it happens. We're going down this little hill, an easy one, and the truck suddenly starts sliding off to the left, farther and farther. Lester's working the clutch, the brake, the gas, the steering wheel, but he still can't stop it from skidding. It was scary, but at least we don't tip over, we just wind up maybe ten feet off the road in a gully. But then we can't get back onto the road. We're stuck there. There's nothing blocking us, but the truck just keeps sliding back."

Just then the teakettle whistled. Uncle Seymour went to the refrigerator, took out a lemon and turned off the kettle.

"You want honey or sugar, I got both."

"Honey, please. Do you want me to help?"

"Sit, I got it. Here's your tea. Watch, it's hot."

"So what happened next?"

"Next we both get out with flashlights to see what the problem is. It's all ice there, under the snow. For an hour and a half we try salt, planks of wood, ropes, tree branches under the wheels. Nothing works. Meanwhile it's blowing snow like crazy. I never saw anything like it. I'm freezing my *tuchas* off. So we get back into the truck to keep warm. Lester tries rocking the truck again, but it's no use.

"We try to figure out what to do. There's no on else out on that *meshuganeh* deer path and the last farmhouse we passed on the way in was about thirty miles from where we're stuck. The Indians are the closest, about fifteen miles away, but they're awfully rough miles and already the snow is over the top of our boots and it's freezing cold, a regular blizzard. So we decide we ain't doing nothing until the storm is over. We'll just stay put. We know we shouldn't waste gasoline, but we got enough to turn the engine on now and then for heat. Plus, Lester's got the jug of Indian moonshine, and he says if we get hungry we can start eating the trees, but then we'll be eating up our profits. Then he says to me maybe I shouldn't eat any trees, they're probably not kosher. A real comic, but I'm not laughing on account of I'm nervous about our situation. Everywhere I look is white stuff and the wind is howling like it's lost its mother. 'Relax,' Lester tells me, 'there's nothing for us to do but wait. And keep warm,' he says and he starts on the jug again.

"So for the next few hours we just sit there, sipping the jug. I guess we both get a little tipsy. Sometimes we talk. We talk about people back home. You know how the mind wanders. We talk about religion. I tell Lester that if we ever get back, he should give a real good tree to his priest, to pick out a nice one. Lester says okay, but he doesn't see why I should contribute a tree to his priest. I tell him it's okay, if my rabbi wants a Christmas tree, we'll give him one, too. Fair is fair.

"I close my eyes and I can just picture Rabbi Bloom—you heard how strict he was—I see him standing next to a Christmas tree like it's a man from Mars. Then I wonder what the Rabbi would say about my new business. After all, where does it say a Jew shouldn't deal in Christmas trees? Maybe this enterprise will allow me to better provide for a family someday. I figure, maybe everything would be all right if I circumcized each tree . An inch off the top. Who would know? Kosher Christmas trees. I could sell them to the whole world, and get money for a down payment on a chain of fancy supermarkets. I would get rich and famous—don't laugh at me, I'm being honest with you—I could then give money to charities, like all the big-shots with their names and pictures in the paper. *That* would make those big-mouths swallow their words. I would be famous for my generosity and they would honor me at ritzy banquets. Why not? It's like they say, only in America.

"Next to me on the seat, Lester is mumbling now from the hootch. He says what we need now is John Wayne and the cavalry to rescue us. He's drunk, he doesn't know what he's saying. I just hope he's not going to get sick on me.

Eventually, he falls asleep with his head against the steering wheel. I take a look around me, it's pitch black so I can't see but I know there's snow all around. It's getting colder and colder. I hope you never know what it's like. I look at my watch, it's one o'clock in the morning and now I feel alone, really alone, like Lester isn't even there with me. I'm scared. Not just about being there or maybe even dying, just scared. There aren't words for it, not in English and not in Yiddish. You know I was never religious. I didn't want to pray for help, I didn't think I was deserving. So I try making imaginary deals with myself, like, if I get home okay I'll donate twenty-five dollars to charity. Why shouldn't I make deals with myself, what have I got to lose? Anyway, the snow still falls and the wind still blows. I make it fifty dollars, then a hundred, then two. The weather gets worse, not better. I'm cold, I'm getting numb all over. I'm getting sleepy, too. I'm feeling bad about making this trip, I never should have gone. They were right, the Felds and Bernstein, Poppa, all of them, it was bad luck to get involved in such a thing. What am I doing with Christmas trees? I'm fed up with myself. I make my last offer: I'll keep on selling the trees every year, but I'll give all my profits to charity, everything, and I'll do it so no one will know it's me—what you call anonymous. Trees, huh? I'll donate all the profits from my trees to *plant* trees in Israel to make the desert bloom. And I'll cut an inch off the top of each Christmas tree. I'm drunk, I'm frozen, I'm hungry, what does it matter what I say? Finally, like a blessing, sleep comes to me.

"When I wake up the next morning my body hurts all over from the cold. We were both lucky we didn't freeze to death, falling asleep like that. The windshields are all frosted over so we can see nothing except that it's light out. We don't hear no wind no more but it's cold, we're both stamping our feet to get the circulation going again. We try opening the doors and they're froze shut. Lester kicks his door open and jumps out. It's not snowing anymore, but the snow comes almost up to his belt and Lester's a big man. That's not just a drift either, it's that way all around us. I jump out in the snow with Lester, and I can't believe it's that deep. It'll take us forever to walk back to the Indians, that's if we make it. We're walking around to inspect the rear of the truck when suddenly I see something moving far away and I strain my eyes and then I yell to Lester, 'Hey Lester, there's your John Wayne!' It's Sidney Bearman and his men with a team of horses to dig us out! We can't believe it. The Indians are wearing showshoes, but I still don't know how the horses ever made it all that way. And Sidney's smiling when he sees us and he's waving to us. 'We figured this would happen to you,' he says with a big grin. They give us some food and coffee from a thermos, then they rig up a hoist to the horses and the men get to shoveling and by and by they get the truck back on the road so the horses can pull it. Sidney rides in the truck with Lester and me and his men guide the horses along for maybe twenty miles, long miles, until we get to where the road is passable without the horses. It takes us almost all day to get those twenty miles. Sidney's already tired from his walk when he found us, so he sleeps most of the way, snoring like he was sawing wood.

"When we get to where the road is good, Lester whispers to me to give the Indians fifty dollars for everything they did for us. Well, we all get out of the truck, then Sidney apologizes for Arthur Goodrich's telling us there wouldn't be any snow, he says Arthur was young and couldn't really know. Sidney takes my phone number so he can call us the next year when *he* knows the weather will be okay. That's when I offer him the fifty dollars, but he won't take any more than twenty-five, just to cover their expenses. Then he winks one of his sad Uncle Hymie eyes at me and he says, "I can't take all this. We couldn't have let anything happen to you. After all, you look like you're going to be a regular customer.'

"You know, after all we went through that time, Lester gave up the Christmas tree business. He said he was lazy, he said it was too hard. Personally, I think he was shook from all that happened to us. So I've kept on doing it all by myself all these years with those same crazy Indians. But let's face it, I'm not a spring chicken any more. What happens to the Indians and the trees after I'm gone?"

Uncle Seymour leaned forward and touched my arm.

"Listen, nephew, how would you like to go into the Christmas tree business?"

Yale Sussman is a freelance writer from Albany, New York. He is presently working on a collection of short stories and on a novel.

"Don't bother to invent any story.
It's obvious that you've been to the movies."

The Lie

BY ANATOLY ALEXIN

GENKA had a predilection for those films which children under
sixteen were not allowed to see. Also, he liked reading books which,
omitting to specify whom they were meant for, were obviously
meant for grownups.

When the radio once announced a lecture for parents, Genka
decided that he just had to listen to it, no matter what.

A flat voice, to which the announcer had attached the important
title of Doctor of Pedagogics, came on the air. Genka always tried to
imagine what the people whose voices he heard over the radio
looked like. Now he conjured up an image of a dry stick of a woman
in pince-nez and white smock. The word *doctor* applied best to her,
because every sentence she uttered sounded like a prescription.

The first prescription was: "The more a child reads, the better he
studies!" That startled Genka, for it meant that he was clearly
growing up in violation of the rules. If he did get a low mark now and

again, it was surely because of the books he read. Until recently, Genka had read at dinner and at supper, using the fat sugar bowl as a prop for his book. At first it stood sedately with its two thin handles akimbo, then it lost one handle, and finally, with Genka's relentless aid, the second.

Nor did the next prescription apply: "The child must respect his parents but never fear them!"

Whereas Genka both respected and feared his father.

It was his father who initially declared war on Genka's "book-swallowing." He went on to the offensive according to all the rules of warfare. First he did some scouting...And it turned out that even the names of the books and their authors were irrevocably muddled in Genka's mind. He confused Cooper with Kuprin, and Stanyukovich with Grigorovich. His father's next move was to plunge into battle, ruthlessly deriding him, even in front of his friends. Genka's defenses cracked, and at this point his father broke through the breach with his main forces.

He dropped his heavy fist on the table, a fist so big that forks and spoons seemed like toys in it.

"From now on we shall read together!"

"What do you mean, together?" Genka asked in surprise. "Out loud?"

"No. But not completely to ourselves either. You will read the books I choose for you, and we'll follow it up with a discussion."

There was a children's library on the first floor of Genka's house. The librarian, a kindly stout woman nicknamed *Don't Tear,* gave Genka the books his father advised him to read.

At supper, the grilling would begin.

"Have you skipped the descriptions of Nature again?"

"N-n-nope!"

"Don't lie! There's nothing worse than lying. To what does the author compare the smell of fresh snow?"

Genka fidgeted in his chair. He wanted to go out and smell the snow so he could find out to what it could be compared.

"The author compares the smell of first snow to the smell of a watermelon! That is a very graphic and apt comparison. And you skipped that place, of course."

Later the exams at suppertime terminated. Instead, there were arguments about books.

Sometimes Genka's mother would join in, and then his father immediately agreed with her. That would make her angry: "Courtesy to women is okay in a streetcar, but not in an argument."

The mother was a typist, and she did her typing at home. She thought that if she left the apartment for a single day something drastic might happen.

Though the mother had nowhere specific to rush off to in the mornings, she got up before anybody, and made breakfast for Genka and his father. When leaving the house, the father kissed her on the top of the head and always said: "So long, baby!"

The mother would flush with pleasure. Genka thought she got up so early just to hear him say those words.

The word "baby" did not suit his mother at all, for she was anything but small. Perhaps she seemed so from the six feet of his father's tremendous height. (Those six feet were Genka's particular pride.) But the father called his little boy sternly and simply by his full name—Gennady.

The father and son left together and walked side by side to the corner.

Genka reveled in walking at his father's side. His mother stayed home, whereas they, like the real men they obviously were, hurried off on business.

Genka knew that all his friends in the yard watched him with envy because they respected his father. It was his dad who had taught the kids to build ice forts, who got the house manager to flood the yard for skating in winter, and who told the boys about the new machines he designed.

They parted at the corner briefly as behooves men of their standing.

"Well, run along," said the father.

In the evening Genka impatiently waited for his father to come home. He immediately recognized his steps. His father climbed the stairs slowly—almost reluctantly—as though wondering, after taking a step, whether to go on or turn back. He would ring the bell once. Genka always wanted to open the door, but he felt that his

161

mother was even more anxious to do it, so he gave in to her. His father would kiss his mother on the top of the head again, saying almost the same words as in the morning: "Lo, baby." But the words were even more caressing, evidently because his father had missed his mother while he was away.

Genka detested endearments, but the words his father said to his mother were like balm to his little heart.

His father then shook his head: "Your eyes are red...Why do you have to bang at that thing all day long?"

"It's not the banging, but my enemies who are to blame," she half-joked. She called the illegible handwriting "her enemies," saying that even at night the unreadable letters would appear in her dreams, particularly the letter "m," which chased her around and around on its three skinny legs.

The father would then say to Genka as though in passing: "Well, how are you getting on in science?"

He never looked at Genka's school diary to see whether the boy was telling the truth. Perhaps that was why Genka couldn't lie. If he came home with a bad mark, he would come out with it straightaway. His father never made any noise about it. Genka had never heard a word of reproach, but neither would he hear, on such evenings, any fascinating stories about sports or the work the engineers were doing which his father, like everybody else, divided into "intelligent" and "unintelligent."

Not so his mother. She opened the diary and looked at the ill-starred mark as though she were reading a death notice. Then she would go to her neighbor's, whose daughter was also in the sixth form, and they would start a conversation in which the names of Genka and the neighbor's daughter were never once mentioned. Instead, Genka's mother spoke of "our boy" and the neighbor of "my girl."

"Our boy brought home *Fair* today. His father said it was worse than *Poor*: neither fish nor fowl," Genka's mother complained. She loved to repeat his father's words, which she always said were the most precise and convincing.

"I wouldn't be so strict if I were you. Your boy has read so many books! My girl won't even open one!"

"No, no, don't try to defend our boy. With his talent, he could be at the head of his class!"

"Ah, but my girl is also very capable."

"Why do all parents think their children are so capable?" Genka wondered. His mother would sigh for a long time afterward. But for Genka, his father's silence was far worse. At such times, Genka would sit down at his homework with particular diligence.

There was only one weakness of Genka's with which his father could not cope. This was his inexhaustible passion for the movies. It seemed that if there were ever pictures prohibited to persons under sixty, Genka would see them anyway. Since he considered sitting anywhere behind the second row an unpardonable luxury, he managed to go to the movies three times on his sixty kopecks! His mother gave him very little money, so he made up the rest by adhering to the most rigid thriftiness: he bought lunch at school only every other day, and rode the subway and the bus without paying for his fare.

Whenever Genka came home all excited and flushed, his father scrutinized him closely, and his eyes would say: "Don't bother to invent any story. It's obvious that you've been to the movies."

At supper, the father would say pensively addressing nobody in particular: "A new picture's on today. I wonder what it's about?"

Genka would willy-nilly have to give a synopsis of the film.

Sometimes his mother said to his father: "How about going to the movies this evening? Genka can get seats for us. He's good at that."

But his father would only spread his arms out guiltily: "I'd love to go, you know that. But this evening I've some pressing thing I've just got to attend to...(Father named one of the "intelligent" engineers with whom he urgently had to get together.)

Genka would give his mother an angry look, as if to say: "Can't you understand how busy Dad is?"

Once Genka heard that an old film was running three blocks from their house, which his friend had said was "great!"

The only reason Genka hadn't seen the film was because it had been made long before he was born.

Most other days, Genka would never have dared to go to an evening show. But this time he knew that his father would be home late, because he had to stay at work for some big occasion—the testing of a new machine. His father had said that something unforeseen might crop up, that one of the "unintelligent" engineers might have something to say against the machine, and that worried him. His father worried! How worried, then, was his mother, as she waited for him to return! In her agitation she couldn't sit still, pecking away at her typewriter for a second, then darting over to the neighbor's, and constantly dashing out onto the landing at the sound of steps...

It was a different story with Genka, who wanted to see the movie to make the hours of expectation go by more quickly, so that when he returned home he would see from the expressions of his father and mother (particularly his mother) that everything was okay, nothing to worry about...

Genka took Zhora, the long-legged seventh-former, with him because Zhora could get tickets to any show. He bought tickets for all the boys in the yard, but not without demanding in return a certain consideration in the form of a rare stamp or a book that was hard to get.

The two boys hurried down the street, colliding with passers-by and muttering hasty pardons which only they themselves could hear. But when they got to the theater, they found that they were too late—all the tickets had been sold. The previous show was over and people were coming out, squinting in the bright lights and pulling on their coats and caps as they exchanged impressions. Genka looked at them with envy.

Suddenly he heard a very familiar voice saying: "You aren't cold, are you baby?"

Genka turned and saw his father. His father was helping a blonde put a bright kerchief on her head.

Genka wanted to turn and run: he had been strictly forbidden to go to evening shows. But he couldn't help raising his eyes and meeting those of his father. He stepped back and gasped—his father looked frightened himself! Yes, yes, his father was frightened! Always so reserved and unhurried in his movements, he now suddenly looked agitated, tugging his hand out of the crook of the blonde's arm and even, as it seemed to Genka, trying to hide behind a pillar which could not conceal him because it was too thin and narrow, and his father too big and broad-shouldered.

Genka made it easier for his father: he bolted so quickly that even long-legged Zhora could hardly keep up with him.

But at the corner he halted for a moment. His ears rang with the words: "You aren't cold, are you baby?" The blonde whom his father had helped with her bright kerchief was really small, but Genka thought it awfully strange that the words that belonged to his mother, and to her alone, could apply to this blonde as well...

What about the machine testing? So it wasn't true? Maybe there wasn't any machine at all? His father had lied! Genka could not understand it. It was just too hard to grasp. Maybe it was all a lie: the talk about books, his father's advice, the arguments at supper. One great big lie?

The librarian nicknamed *Don't Tear* called out to him: "Genka, come on in. I have the book you were looking for."

But Genka only waved a hand. He didn't want the book his father had advised him to read. He couldn't believe in the book now.

As soon as he got home he went to bed.

"What's the matter, child, you're so hot...Are you running a temperature?" his mother asked in alarm.

"Don't worry, Mom. I'm just tired," Genka said, as gently as always.

He didn't want to hear—he didn't think he could bear hearing—what his father would say when his mother opened the door.

Born in 1924 in Moscow, Anatoly Alexin has become well-known to Soviet readers. His works have been translated into many languages of the USSR nationalities and other countries. He has been nominated for a USSR State Prize for several of his short stories. He is a winner of the RSFSR State Prize and Secretary of the Board of the RSFSR Writers' Union. A number of his plays have been staged. The story was translated by L. Flaxman.

Coming up in future issues of SSI

USA	**Irwin Shaw** Mixed Doubles
Western Samoa	**Albert Wendt** Birthdays
Ireland	**T.G. Nestor** The Standing Stone
England	**E.G. Peacock** Swings and Roundabouts
Korea	**Kim Tongni** Picture of a Sorceress
Germany (GDR)	**Werner Bergengruen** The Mysterious Typewriter
Scotland	**Roderick Wilkinson** The Bidders
USSR (Chukotka)	**Yuri Ritkheu** Kakot's Numbers
Australia	**James McQueen** Love and Goldfish
Belgium	**Albert Russo** The Age of the Pearl
USA	**Mark Helprin** Palais de Justice
Spain	**Robert Culff** The Closing of the Season
South Africa	**Jane Meiring** Rendezvous
Singapore	**Rebecca Chua** The Newspaper Editor
Czechoslovakia	**Pavel Francouz** The Case of the Mercedes
Mexico	**Carlos Fuentes** A Pure Soul

And, for your reading pleasure, other intriguing,
insightful stories from all lands.

For readers who can't read...

Greek, Arabic, Chinese, Japanese, Dutch, Norwegian, Chukchi, Finnish, Hindi, Turkish, Urdu, Hebrew, Russian, Vietnamese, Portugese, etc., etc.

Short Story International takes you to all points of the compass, to anywhere in the world. There are intriguing stories waiting for you in future issues of SSI—stories that will involve you in corners of this world you've never seen . . . and in worlds outside of this one . . . with glimpses into the future as well as the past, revealing fascinating, universal truths that bypass differences in language and point up similarities in peoples.

Send in the coupon below and every other month SSI will take you on a world cruise via the best short stories being published throughout the world today—the best entertainment gleaned from the work of the great creative writers who are enhancing the oldest expression of the entertainment arts—the short story.